VEILS

SHORT STORIES

NAHID RACHLIN

CITY LIGHTS BOOKS
SAN FRANCISCO

Cover design by John Miller, Big Fish/Books
Back cover: Photograph of Nahid Rachlin by Howard Rachlin

The stories in *Veils* first appeared in somewhat different form
in the following journals: "Fanatics" in *Ararat*, "Rahbar" in
Pleiades, "Departures" in *City Lights Review*, "The Son" in
Ararat, "The Poet's Visit" in *Redbook*, "Fatemeh" in *Ararat*,
"Dark Gravity" in *Confrontation*, "The Calling" in *Shenandoah*,
and "Dreamers" in *North Atlantic Review*.
"Without My Sister, Would I Have Become a Writer" was
published in *The Confidence Woman*.

Library of Congress Cataloging-in-Publication Data

Rachlin, Nahid.
    Veils : short stories / by Nahid Rachlin.
       p.   cm.
    ISBN 0-87286-267-4 : $8.95
    1. Iranian Americans—Fiction.   I. Title.
  PS3568.A244V4   1992
813'.54—dc20   92-218
                                          CIP

City Lights Books are available to bookstores through our
primary distributor: Subterranean Company. P. O. Box 160,
265 S. 5th St., Monroe, OR 97456. 503-847-5274. Toll-free
orders 800-274-7826. FAX 503-847-6018. Our books are also
available through library jobbers and regional distributors. For
personal orders and catalogs, please write to City Lights Books,
261 Columbus Avenue, San Francisco, CA 94133.

CITY LIGHTS BOOKS are edited by Lawrence Ferlinghetti and
Nancy J. Peters and published at the City Lights Bookstore,
261 Columbus Avenue, San Francisco, CA 94133.

For my sister Pari

TABLE OF CONTENTS

FANATICS

1

As I sit here in my dormitory room my mind keeps circling obsessively to my friend Farzaneh. In a photograph of her I took out of a box filled with old pictures and letters, she is strikingly pretty — slender and tall, her long, dark hair parted in the middle. But is there something frantic, desperate, about her expression that I had missed in it before? Each time I look I see something different. At one moment she appears to be brimming with hope, at another despairing, and at another totally blank as though no longer existing in the framework of her own body. In a letter she wrote to me a while back she says, " . . . I'm more and more disillusioned with everything. It's like being inside of an airless box with the lid tightly shut. My father is still trying to make me into who he thinks I should be, marry a man he likes (my last suitor was a rich, stuffy man my father's age). How lucky you are to have left Iran . . . "

Lucky.

How many times have I read her father's letter I received in the mail today?

"Dear Manijeh,

"You may be surprised to get a letter from me but you of all people should know about this — your friend was arrested, while walking home from shopping, on the charge of subversive activities as a member of the Ijtemah party, and was put into jail. It is as if hell has descended on us already on this earth. I am writing partly to seek your help. Can you tell me anything you might know about her friendships and associations that might show authorities that she was innocent. She is in the women's section of Evin prison . . . "

Farzaneh, only twenty-one years old and in jail. She had had so much.

My eyes drift back to the letter again. "I am permitted to visit her once a week for precisely fifteen minutes while a guard stands beside us. She is not allowed to receive any letters or packages, so do not try to write to her. It could only get her into trouble. She has lost a lot of weight already, her face is sallow. They could be torturing her — her arms and neck were covered. From when she was a child I gave her everything she wanted. She was a wonderful girl but something got into her. She refused to get married, although she had many suitors. She said she did not ever want to get married or have children. It is never going to be the same for me here. The house is empty without her . . . "

I remember passing Evin Prison not long before I left for the United States, when I had gone to the central section of Teheran to get a passport photograph — a gray, grim building, its courtyard choked with crouching old trees, silhouettes of prisoners hovering behind its dust-covered, opaque windows, strange, sad murmurs coming out of it.

Sometimes when I visited Farzaneh the two of us would sit by the large pool in their elegant garden and talk. We would stare at the goldfish with hopes that one of them would suddenly turn magical and say, "Come with me, I know the way!"

Neither of us had any specific idea what another world would encompass. We just wanted an atmosphere where we would float on the top of blue waves, to freedom.

It was impossible not to notice her in the crowded school yard. She wore expensive clothes and jewelry. She could get away with a lot — skip classes, occasionally not wear the uniform required at school — because her father was the president of the University of Teheran. Sometimes she avoided everyone, was moody, sometimes she would mingle with others to talk about a book she had just finished or a movie she had seen. She never stayed with one group for very long.

I think of the day our friendship started. All the students in the high school were standing in lines in front of classrooms. Miss Davaran came over to the line I was standing in and began to inspect us. "Your nails," I could hear her from behind me. "They need to be cut." "Your collar isn't tucked in properly." "That's good, I see your face is scrubbed, none of that make-up." I knew she was talking to Farah, because Farah was caught wearing make-up a few days ago and was forced to go to the principal's office.

Miss Davaran reached me. She looked at my nails, face, and then to my relief she went on. She passed by Farzaneh, who was standing right in front of me, without inspecting her. My eyes caught Farzaneh's. She smiled in an almost rueful, guilty way.

Then our attention was caught by Miss Davaran standing in front of the line and saying, "I have an announcement to make."

A hush fell over everyone.

"There have been reports that two or three of our students — I don't want to name them — have been responding to boys who loiter around our school, boys who put letters into your hands or try to lure you to meet them. I know you're all young and innocent, and may be tempted, but just remember being caught in such conduct, which is in deep violation of our religion and laws, will jeopardize your place in school. And then you will also have to answer to the authorities above us . . . "

The bell rang and the line began to move toward the classroom.

Farzaneh came and sat next to me. I opened my book to the page where the last lesson began. I tried to visualize the foreign places described in the book. All I could see were immense fields with low green hills surrounding them, streams running into one another, women with large hats and elegant long skirts walking on the streets. Everything was vast, peaceful. Then some of the images became more specific. London: lost like a small gray stone in layers of fog. New York: a revolving globe with columns of colored light reflected on its surface. I heard the teacher asking, "What is one of Denmark's exports?" No one answered. She turned to Farzaneh.

"Eh . . . " Farzaneh mumbled.

"Does anyone know the answer?"

"Sardines," I said.

"Very good," the teacher said, making a few jittering steps to and fro.

"What is the capital of Argentina?" she asked.

Again no one volunteered. I said, "Buenos Aires."

She nodded.

I was aware that Farzaneh was looking at me with strange scrutiny, having always lumped me with the less privileged students at school, with my cheap gray uniform, my hair always brushed back plainly and covered by a kerchief. She must have noticed that I took the bus toward the older, less fashionable part of town.

At the end of that day, she came over to me and said, in a half-jesting manner, "You know your geography."

"I have to know about other countries. I want to leave this country after high school, if I manage to get a scholarship at a university."

She looked astonished.

"I want to be somewhere bigger."

"Do you want to come over to my house today and study together?"

"Not today," I said. "But maybe some other time."

"How about tomorrow?"

Her house, located on the other side of the city from mine, was set off from other houses of university employees by a narrow path with a profusion of trees. In the center of its well-kept garden, her father was playing ping-pong with another man. They stopped playing as they saw us approach. Farzaneh introduced me to her father and he introduced his friend. Her father was very handsome and exuded self-confidence.

"I've been eager to meet one of Farzaneh's friends," he said. "I'm afraid my daughter keeps too much to herself." He put his hand around Farzaneh and squeezed her arm. Then he and his friend went back to playing ping-pong.

I followed Farzaneh to her room.

Her room was expensively furnished as I had expected, with a plush white rug on the floor, a cherrywood bed and desk, a TV, a phonograph with many records on a shelf next to it. It had several large windows overlooking the garden, with flowering bushes set close to the house, below the room. Her closet was full of pretty, glamorous-looking clothes. I was filled with shame at the thought of my own room — small, covered by a rug in subdued colors, no desk, no phonographs or luxuries — and of my own plain clothes made by my mother. And then at the thought of my parents, neither one of them having gone beyond grade school: my father who worked at a bakery, my mother who taught the Koran to the neighborhood children for a small amount of money. My brother had stopped going to high school a year ago and worked with my father. They came home in sweaty, ragged clothes. I could never invite Farzaneh to my house.

"Would you like something to drink?" she asked. "Coke, lemonade?"

"Lemonade."

She left the room.

I noticed the photograph of a woman, in a silver frame, hanging on the wall above her desk. She was wearing an elegant red dress, which attractively outlined her slender figure. She had the same features as Farzaneh, large gray eyes, full lips, long wavy hair. She must be Farzaneh's mother. It was the expression on the woman's face, though, that rivetted my eyes on her. There was something entranced about it, remote, as if she were sleepwalking.

"That's my mother," Farzaneh said. She had come back into the room. She gave me the tall glass jingling with ice. We both sat down on chairs she set across from each other. "I can hear her voice still, singing to me, feel her touch when she gave something to me." Tears gathered in her eyes.

Was her mother dead?

"But let's not talk about her," she said.

We started to do homework, frequently pausing to gossip about the other students or teachers.

There was a knock on the door and then her father said, "Dinner is ready."

"I should be going," I said.

"Why don't you stay for dinner, then the chauffeur will take you back."

"We're coming," Farzaneh said to her father.

In a few moments she took me to the dining room. The table was already set for three. The pink silk curtains were drawn over the windows. Two candles in brass holders were burning on the table.

She sat down and I sat next to her awkwardly, while her father sat across from us.

A maid walked in with a tray of food. She arranged the food on the table and walked away.

"Well, what do you expect to do when you graduate from high school?" her father asked me.

"I want to go abroad."

He looked at me with the same astonishment as his daughter had. "Oh?" he said as if I were merely fantasizing.

"My parents have no idea about my goal but I'll be able to convince them to let me go if I get into a college with a scholarship."

"I see," he said.

"That's what I want to do, go to Europe or America," Farzaneh said, addressing me. "But my father . . . " She turned to him. "Tell her what your objection is."

"I don't believe we should let our young people leave the country. I've been trying to improve the educational system. My daughter should stay on and help me with that. I must admit to a selfish motive too. I have only one daughter, I don't want to lose her. Almost all the young people who go abroad end up staying, marrying someone there. I don't want that to happen. And with her mother's condition . . . "

A palpable tension hung in the air.

"Did Farzaneh mention it to you?"

"No," Farzaneh replied for me.

"Well, you shouldn't avoid talking about it." He turned to me again. "Her mother has been suffering from mental illness. More and more the doctors believe it's congenital. The best we can do is keep her from harming herself. She's in a hospital."

Mental illness. How sad, strange. Poor Farzaneh.

Farzaneh was looking downward, sorrow — or was it shame — spreading over her face.

"I need my daughter in Iran," he said with emphasis.

After we had dessert Farzaneh's father got up. "I have to go out now." He said goodbye and left.

Farzaneh and I went into the garden. We sat on a wooden bench and took off our shoes, cooling our feet in the little stream running by. A cool breeze was blowing through the trees.

"My poor mother is locked up in a hospital, probably for the rest of her life," she said. "Before she was hospitalized she had gotten hold of a pair of scissors and cut off all her hair and then she came into my room and cut off some of mine. I screamed and screamed . . . "

We were quiet for a moment. Then she said, "But you know, sometimes I feel I'm locked up, like she is, in this house, by my father . . . I want to tell you something. You promise you won't tell anyone?"

"I promise."

"I have been secretly meeting this boy, Jalal. He's so nice."

From behind the trees the chauffeur appeared, coming toward us. "Do you want a ride home?" he asked me.

"He leaves at this time," Farzaneh explained.

"It's time for me to go anyway," I said, getting up.

Farzaneh came with us to the gate. As I was getting into the Mercedes I watched her walking back on the path between two rows of trees. I was vividly aware of her loneliness.

Saiid and I were silent as he drove and then I got off several blocks before reaching our alley so that he would not see what kind of a neighborhood I lived in. I walked along the unfamiliar street, ashamed of my own shame. A row of houses stood on each side of the street, making it seem very narrow, like a tunnel. The setting sun had reached the chimney tops and tall trees. I began to become concerned and started walking faster.

When I reached our house I found my brother standing at the door. "Oh, you're back finally," he said. "You know a young girl shouldn't be out at this hour."

I walked past him brusquely and went into my room, shutting the door behind me.

2

Farzaneh came to school late the next day. The history class had been in session for ten minutes or so when she arrived and sat next to me. The teacher was talking about the Persian and Greek wars. "Xerxes watched the battle from his silver-footed throne at the base of the hill. Victory was in sight but soon after, the Athenians sunk two hundred Persian ships . . . " I was distracted by a piece of paper Farzaneh put in front of me. On it she had written, "My father gave me hell because Saiid saw me with Jalal."

I scribbled at the bottom of the sheet, "Be careful," and put it back in front of her. We kept passing notes like that back and forth.

When the class ended we dashed out and went toward the large, empty field behind the school. We sat on the steps of a half-demolished building, which eventually was going to be made into an auditorium. It was cool out and shadows around us were long and still as if they were drawn carefully with a stencil. Pale sunshine glinted at the top of the bare trees.

"My father kept saying, didn't I know the consequences for a girl to be intimate with a boy she isn't even engaged to?" Farzaneh said. "I'm really getting afraid of my father, that he'll lock me up like he did my mother."

"But your mother . . . "

"I know she has to be hospitalized. But then you can always construe any behavior you don't like as insanity."

I felt a chill on my skin that went beyond the cool air, her voice was so dark and bleak.

"Do you visit her?" I asked.

"The hospital is hours away from Teheran. I've been there a few times. Each time I come back devastated." She kept kicking a pebble with her foot. She stopped suddenly and said, "I dreamt about Mother last night. She was sitting at the edge of my bed, singing, like when I was a child. And then she leaned over me and said, in the same way you're talking, 'Be careful.' Before I had a chance to say anything she disappeared. I sat up in my bed and kept looking around for her, I couldn't believe it was just a dream. Then I started to cry."

"What are you going to do about Jalal, with your father's objections?"

"I'll be more careful."

3

For several days Farzaneh did not come to school at all. The few times I called her I had not been able to reach her and I did not have a phone so she couldn't call me back.

I tried to spend more time with my other friends. One, Zahra, was among the few students like myself whose parents were not able to afford our private school, and she came there on a scholarship like I did. She also dressed as plainly as I did.

"Is Farzaneh sick?" she asked me as I joined her in the yard at the recess.

"She has a bad case of the flu."

"If I were you, I would stay away from her," she said abruptly. "You know how she's been acting."

When the last class ended I decided to go to Farzaneh's house. After several days of snow the sun had come out. The fine, thin layer of snow, covering everything was rapidly melting. I pulled up the collar of my coat and wrapped the scarf around my head tightly and went toward the Square to take a bus to her house.

The gate was open and I went inside. The garden was empty and silent, the statues looking as if they were meditating on the beauty around them. I heard footsteps approaching from behind and I turned around. It was Saiid.

"Is Farzaneh in?" I asked.

"Yes, she's in her room. She'll be happy to see you. Go ahead and knock."

I went up the stairs, a sense of foreboding sweeping over me. I knocked on the door and waited. There was no answer. Saiid had followed me up the stairs. He said, "Farzaneh *khanoom*, it's your friend, Manijeh."

"Come in," I heard Farzaneh's voice, very softly. "The door is open."

As I was going inside Saiid walked away. The room was dim, with only rays of late afternoon sunlight skipping in through the drawn curtains. I could barely make out her shape on the bed, under a blanket. "Farzaneh, what's happening? I've been worried."

As I went closer I could see she was not her usual self. Her skin was ashen, she had dark circles under her eyes.

"It has been hell." She sat up on the bed. She was wearing a lacy nightgown and her hair hung in coils over it. "I spent the whole day in bed. Did you hear about Jalal?"

"No, what?"

She leaned over, turned on the lamp on the side table, and took from the drawer a folded sheet torn out of a newspaper. She handed it to me.

I opened it and immediately noticed the large headline. "Demonstration Against the Education Minister . . . " Underneath was a photograph of a man who was holding a banner and surrounded by a mob. He was very attractive in a thin, intense way.

"That's him. My father said Jalal is his enemy. He's doing things against the education system."

"Isn't it better for you to stop seeing Jalal for now?"

"How can I just stop it? I really admire him, what he stands for. He makes me feel guilty about all the luxury I live in."

She spoke in a ponderous, heavy manner. As if looking at two photographs, I could compare her image now to the heedlessness and exuberance she projected the first time I had seen her, the first day I came to Farhangi School. As I had entered the school yard that day Farzaneh was talking with a group of other students and laughing a lot. She looked utterly carefree . . .

Farzaneh got out of the bed and went to the mirror. She kept looking at herself, as if at a new person. She pulled up her hair at the top, slanted her eyes with her fingers. "I look strange, don't I?" she said.

There was a knock at the door. "May I take you home?" It was Saiid's voice, obviously addressing me.

"I guess I should go. But please, come back to school. You're destroying your own future," I whispered to Farzaneh.

She just shook her head. I left the room and then followed Saiid to the car parked near the gate.

Again I got out of the car several blocks before my house. And again, as I approached our neighborhood, I was keenly aware of its barrenness and squalor — beggars sitting or sleeping on the steps of the mosques, nothing to do at night — except for a few tea houses in which mostly men sat around smoking waterpipes — no theaters, bookstores. And none of the young girls I knew were aiming for an education.

At home my father and mother were entertaining a man in the living room, I could see them through the half-open door. He was middle-aged, thin, had reddish patches on his cheeks. His distinct, dark eyebrows and dark eyes looked as if they were carefully drawn on his face. My mother came out of the room. "Will you bring in some *sharbat* to serve him?" she asked me, winking. "He's here for you."

He was obviously a suitor and I found myself blushing.

"His mother and sister have already seen you on the way home from school and now he's here to have a look at you. He makes good money, comes from a respectable family."

"Mother, I'm not cattle."

"Stop talking like that."

"I'm going away from this house, this country." I stomped my foot and dashed into my room.

4

There is a knock on my door. "Come in," I say, looking up from the letters on my desk.

The door opens and Janis walks in. She looks dishevelled with no make-up on — a little like Farzaneh on that day — the robe wrapped around her is stained with coffee.

"I came in to see if you want to do something tonight."

"Can I let you know later?"

"You work too hard."

"I have to."

"You should make some time for fun."

Another time she told me, in passing, that I am too serious. "All right, I'll take tonight off."

After she leaves I look at myself in the mirror. Am I too earnest looking, a grind? My face reflects back someone sober. But I can't change a lifetime of habits, experiences.

Then I begin to think of other students in this college who are restless and depressed. Last week a student in the dormitory jumped off the bridge into the stream below. That spot on the campus normally radiates gaiety. During the day the surface of the stream reflects the sun and at night the moon and the stars. Birds dive into the water, sing in the trees surrounding it. Yet time after time a young man or a woman standing on the spot can only think about the pain throbbing inside them. They see only darkness, a hopeless monotony, unremitting loneliness. I remember how elated I was getting ready to come here. A joyful tune reverberated inside of me all the time. That tune rarely starts up in me these days. Everything has leveled off somehow . . . What does it all mean then?

The dormitory is quiet. The students are either out or sitting in their rooms studying. I put my books away and begin to get ready to go out and meet Janis. I need to get out. I have been dwelling too much on the past. In an attempt to seem less serious I comb my hair and let it hang loose over my shoulders, apply make-up to my face, and put on a pair of dangling earrings. Then I pick up my pocketbook and leave my room.

On the way out I stop in the mail room to see if I have any letters, always hoping for something from Iran. On the bulletin board in the mailroom I notice an announcement for a memorial service in the school chapel on Sunday for Cynthia Peterson, the student from my dorm who had committed suicide. I pause there for a moment, reading the announcement more than once. "We invite you to gather in St. Patrick's Chapel at 12 noon on Sunday, April 22, to solemnly commiserate with Cynthia Peterson's family." I walk away to check my mail. Nothing important. I go out and walk along College Street. The lamps cast a yellowish glow on everything. Other students are passing by on foot or bicycles, talking, laughing, on the tree-lined street. They come and go as they please. I come and go as I please. When I reach The Park Bench, bright with neon lights, I see Janis is sitting inside with Jack and Michael, two other juniors, drinking beer and talking. She must have come across them there by chance and decided to join them. I know she has a crush on Michael. I like Jack, though I don't understand him — with his baseball hats and his constant reference to old movies and his slang that I cannot follow with my barely fluent English. On the door of his room he has pasted a sticker saying, "LIVE FAST, DIE YOUNG, AND MAKE A GOOD LOOKING CORPSE."

I join them and also order beer. We talk randomly about this and that, nothing serious, and I manage to throw myself into the flow of the conversation.

"Do you want to see a movie?" Jack asks, addressing all of us.

"What's playing?" I ask.

"We can look."

The movie we end up seeing is *The Big Chill*. We talk heatedly about it as we walk back to the dormitories. Even Jack now is somber, serious, discussing the suicide in the movie.

"Did you know Cynthia, on the second floor? Her memorial service is on Sunday," I say to Jack.

"I knew her, yes."

"Do you know what was going on?"

"No. I thought she was happy."

"She must have been pretending," Janis says.

"No one can pretend so well for so long. I knew her from last year. I know her brother too. He goes to school with my brother. He said his sister had fewer problems than he did."

"She must have had a reason though," I say.

We have reached the complex of dormitories at the end of College Street. Janis and Michael say goodbye and go toward her room on the first floor of our dormitory.

"I'll walk you to your room," Jack says and follows me up the stairs.

At the door he says, "You're really pretty when you smile." After a pause he adds, "I'll talk to you soon." Then he leaves.

I lie in bed, thinking of the way the stars were shining the last night I was home as I lay, unable to sleep, under the mosquito netting on the rooftop. I think of the cool dampness of the water jug I had taken up with me, and how I lifted it up to take a few gulps of water. The hum of insects mingling with the faraway sounds coming from a mosque that stayed open all night.

And I thought of the last day before I left. The air was hazy with a cloud of dust and people had sunk into apathy; my mother, father, and brother took me to the airport.

As we waited for my flight, my father said, as if he still was not sure, "I had to let you go. So go and do something good, useful."

My brother said, "You're doing what I should have done." He kept his face downward, a habit he had of rarely looking at people when he spoke.

My mother said, with tears in her eyes, "When you get lonely there, just sit down and write a long letter to us."

I remember smiling at what they said, thinking to myself I was escaping. Yes, escape was the most pronounced feeling I had.

5

In the mailbox I find a letter postmarked Iran, with Farzaneh's home address. Probably from her father again. Did my vague answer to his letter, denying I knew anything, make him want to write again? I walk rapidly toward my room to read it there, in solitude.

I put down my heavy book bag, sit down at the edge of the bed, covered by an Iranian bedspread with busy paisley and floral designs, and tear open the letter. I find only a cutting from a newspaper in it.

" . . . It has been established by the police that one of the three women whose car ran into the Ministry of Education in a suicide attack was Farzaneh Yahyai, the daughter of Mahmood Yahyai, the president of the University of

Teheran. She and two other inmates of Evin Prison escaped last night with help from a group calling themselves Ijtemah that had also provided them with the car and the bomb. Part of the building was destroyed, and many people critically injured. All three in the car were killed . . . "

My mind keeps circling around one image: Farzaneh sitting in that car, her body taut with anger, her eyes looking around cautiously as she waits for the exact moment. Perhaps floating across her mind are those images of blue waves on which she and I used to imagine we'd ride into another realm. Did she falter when the moment arrived to set the bomb off, was she tempted to abandon the project before it was too late? I think of her suicide and Cynthia's. Is there any difference?

A leaf blows in, bobs around the air, and settles on the floor. I pick it up and play with it aimlessly. White clouds are rushing across the sky before the window, as they did that first day I went home with Farzaneh, when she was still alive.

FATEMEH

Fatemeh put her *chador* on and left her room early in the morning. She had a lot to do that day. In the alley, sweepers were going around with brooms, cleaning. At the curb of the alley a *hejleh* was set up, a bunch of tiny bulbs lit inside its glass case and an enlarged photograph of a young man pasted on its front. "Gholam, 18, martyred in the holy war," was written in red ink beneath the photograph. Tears gathered in her eyes. Will I be able to get Ali exempted; will God pay back my prayers, the pilgrimages I went on for a whole year, she wondered. It was wonderful last night, staring at the face of the moon, as she lay under the mosquito netting on the roof, seeing something, a trembling light, which had made her feel God was showing a bit of Himself to her. That had excited her so much that she had sat up and stared for a long time at the moon, for more signs. The sky was dazzling, with all the stars, large and clear . . .

On Ghanat Abad Avenue there was another *hejleh* right next to the beet stall. The man in the stall was shouting, "I have the best, sweetest beets in town, they taste like sugar." Doesn't he see that *hejleh*, she thought indignantly.

She walked rapidly toward the bus station. In the station she bought a ticket and got on the bus which was about to leave for Ghom. She sat by the window looking out but her mind was filled with all those weeks of going from office to office until she had gotten an appointment with Ayatollah Masjedi about Ali, then the meeting they had in the mosque.

"Don't you want your son to give himself up to the holy cause? His soul will directly go into heaven, if he's martyred. All the sins either one of you might have committed will be forgiven by God. What is the brief, wretched life we lead on this earth compared to a blissful eternity in heaven?" the ayatollah had said.

"Ayatollah Masjedi, he's my only son. I have a daughter, but I haven't seen her since she was eight years old, her father took her away from me . . . I had two other sons, they died. I can't let this one go. I have no one else in the world. Anyway he supports me. I do all I can cleaning house for rich people, but it only pays for our rent."

"Well then," he said. "Do you have proof that he's your only son?"

His tone was mild but Fatemeh was cut by an expression of utter disgust on his desiccated face.

"I can get proof," she stammered.

He waved his hand stiffly, dismissing her. The veins on his neck were drawn taut, his eyes were stony.

Am I going to be able to get proof today from that man in the morgue? Who knows if he is still there, or if he remembers anything. Would he have a record of my two little boys' deaths after all these years? All the possible complications . . .

"I'm really running away from my husband," she heard the woman sitting on the seat in front of her saying to another woman next to her. "He's truly frightening, the way he goes into a rage and starts throwing things at me . . . "

I was so frightened of my husbands, Fatemeh thought, of all three — Majid, Bahram, Khosro. Bastards. One she had left, giving up all claim to money; another all claim to money and worse — he had taken her only daughter, Nasrin, with him, had hidden her from her, forbidden visits, and then vanished leaving no trace. And of course the law was on his side. She was the one who had left. Ali's father, her first husband, was not such a bad man, only he was a drug addict, and though he had never abused her, he was useless. At least she had managed to get her son back from him. But first the poor boy had had to put up with the two stepfathers, then his half-sister to whom he had grown attached was taken away. The most joyous moments of my life were when I was pregnant, she thought. And how magical it was when the midwife would hold up the infant to her, then lay it into her arms. The feeling she had then was like looking at the moon last night and being aware of God. She would put her breast into the baby's mouth, hold its soft, small hand or foot, tickle its belly. Nasrin was a precocious baby, began to walk and talk early. On hot days she put her in a plastic pool and Nasrin splashed around or pushed the ball floating on its surface.

What was happening to her now? She may be married, have children of her own . . .

She got off the bus in Ghom and after she had walked a few blocks she recalled where the mortuary was. She started in its direction. The streets were crowded and dirty, the trees and buildings dust-covered. Many *Agh-ounds* were passing by in their long robes and turbans.

The mortuary was a grim looking house on a quiet, rather deserted street. She knocked several times on the door and waited. There were tiny termite holes in the door. The few houses and shops on the street were in a bad state, some of their roofs or windows shattered. She heard footsteps from the inside and an old man opened the door.

"Yes," he said. He had yellowish crooked teeth. There was something deeply bitter in his expression.

"I have to talk to you about my two children I brought here."

"When was that?"

"It was years ago but . . . "

He seemed to be about to shut the door on her.

"Please, it's very important, I have to have proof that they died, please let me explain."

With a reluctant air he let her in.

Inside, in the dim light, she could see coffins lying around. There was a raised pool in the corner with several faucets and a cemented platform next to it, where they washed dead bodies before they wrapped them up in cloths and put them in coffins to be taken to the cemetery. She began to shudder — she could see so vividly the small bodies of her children being washed in that very pool, floating like dolls.

The man plopped himself on a wooden bench as if he were exhausted. She sat down also.

"What do you want *khanoom*, maybe you can tell me something to refresh my memory."

"What can I tell you. The last one I brought here was Mohsen; he was five years old; he got malaria. I had my little girl with me also when we came here. She was frightened and she clung to me the whole time and cried. Now I remember something. There was a fly buzzing around in the air. You told my daughter that the fly was the soul of her brother. She was startled by what you told her and stopped crying. Do you remember?"

He scratched his head, coughed. "Oh, Mohsen, sure, in fact not long ago, a man and a woman came here and asked me about him, they couldn't find the grave. They must have been your husband and daughter then. I told them where the grave was."

Her heart almost jumped out of her chest. "They were here? Where did they come from?"

He looked at her in a puzzled way.

"Do they live in Ghom? You see he's no longer my husband. He has kept my daughter from me."

"Oh, you poor woman."

"I have only one son living with me, from my first husband. He was a gift to me . . . and now they're going to draft him unless I can prove that I have no other sons or a husband who support me. Will you write a letter about my two sons being buried by you? If you would do me that favor, I'm sure God will pay you back. I can pay you with what I can, which is only some *tomans*." She fumbled in her purse and found the hundred *toman* bill which she had just gotten for some housework she had done. She needed it for her next month's rent but she could see him opening up to the idea so she gave it to him. He took it without hesitation and put it into his gray, frayed jacket pocket.

He got up slowly and went to the heavy wooden table in a corner and sat on a chair behind it. He began to write a letter with a pen he dipped in ink. After a moment he handed it to her.

"This is to certify that Mohsen . . . " He indicated both names, dated and signed it.

"I can't thank you enough," she said.

"I can tell you where the graves are. In fact there are fresh flowers on them. I do my duty — your daughter wanted me to put flowers on them every week. She's been sending me money for it. Go inside the cemetery and walk past the three graves with the very large, upright stones on them. Your sons' graves are just beyond them."

"Did my daughter or . . . her father . . . tell you where they were living right now, any addresses?"

He thought for a moment. "The money for flowers comes from Teheran."

They live in Teheran then, she thought. How incredible. She took out another bill, this time twenty *tomans,* and gave it to him. "Could you give me the address?"

He looked through some papers scattered on the top of the desk and in the drawers, and picked out one. He gave it to her. "Here, is this the name?"

"Oh yes, that's my daughter's name, how incredible." The address was the old house where they had all lived, a house Bahram had inherited from his parents. So he had returned there. Was Nasrin living with him, with a husband maybe?

After she left, though, instead of going to the cemetery she headed back home. It is more important to attend to those still living, she thought. If she went to the cemetery she would miss the only bus going back to Teheran today and she would have to stay overnight. She could not afford the money or the time. As she headed toward the bus she was elated — it seemed she had accomplished an incredible amount.

In the morning, she decided to go to the War-Related-Matters office first and submit the letter and her divorce documents and then from there go to see if she could track down Nasrin in the old house.

The office was teeming with people — parents, young men. Most of them seemed anxious. From what they were saying, some of the young men were there to enlist, some of the parents to collect compensations. Fatemeh was anxious too, aware of hot and cold flashes on her skin. A large bowl, filled with *sharbat,* was set in a corner next to some glasses and people went over and helped themselves to the drink. It was clearly going to be hours of waiting. She was such an insignificant figure, one among so many others, like a pale line on a white sheet of paper. The woman sitting next to her said, "I don't know what's happening to my son. I haven't heard from him for weeks and there are no reports on him. I haven't been able to find out anything about him."

A name was called and the woman jumped to her feet. "That's me." She walked away with choppy steps. Her black *chador,* which she held tightly around her, was too long, hindering her.

Finally, hours later, Fatemeh was called in. The man sitting behind the desk was short, bald, there was a pinched meanness about his face.

"Yes," he said curtly.

Fatemeh fumbled in her purse. She took out the documents and put them before him. "I had the privilege of meeting with Ayatollah Masjedi. He told me these are what I need."

"Your name?"

"Fatemeh Abbasi."

He began to look at the documents. She had a sinking, helpless feeling.

"We'll send you a letter about our decision," he said finally, after an eternity.

"Please, could you tell me now?"

"We'll send you a letter," he repeated impatiently.

What am I going to find, what can I expect from a child I haven't seen for so long, a woman now, but clearly a nice person to want to send flowers to her brother who died years ago. Has she been missing me? But if she hasn't contacted me all this time, living in Teheran, her mind must have been poisoned against me. The thoughts went around her head as she went toward the house in Varamin, where they used to live. What is Bahram like now? Is he as erratic, volatile as he used to be? He is capable of tender feelings toward his children, why not toward a wife? Bastard. As she reached Ghole Sar Lane, on which the house was located, she was so overwhelmed by contradictory feelings that she almost turned around and went back. She had to push herself to go on.

Then she was in front of the house and knocking. There were no sounds from the inside. Maybe no one was in. Bahram would be at his job, if he had one. Grape vines were hanging on the crude brick and straw wall. She knocked again. Then she heard footsteps in the hall and the door was opened by a woman. Nasrin. A grown woman, but she had the same features as the child she remembered.

"Do you know who I am?" Fatemeh asked through constricted throat.

Nasrin shook her head. "Can I help you?"

There was something sweet and kind in Nasrin's manner.

"Nasrin, my dear, I'm your mother."

"My mother?" A range of emotions passed over her face. "Really . . . my mother. Come in now, come in."

Fatemeh went down the two steps and they embraced, for a long moment. She wished she could hold her daughter forever. At some level she had a hard time believing it was really happening, that she was not merely dreaming it. How could she be holding her, finding her so easily, after years of having no idea where she was? Then in the midst of her emotions she felt a stab of guilt, thinking, maybe I really was not trying. Maybe I was afraid of encountering Bahram. But she said, "I thought you had moved away."

"We had. We came back here, this was rented until a few months ago. I'll tell you everything, if you come in and sit down."

Fatemeh followed Nasrin into the living room. They sat on a rug and talked. A few times they reached over and kissed each other. Once they both burst out crying.

The house was the same, only older, more run down. Just being there, being reminded of all the abuse Bahram had inflicted on her — she still had a scar on her chin from when he had thrown a plate at her — made her want to get up and leave but then there was Nasrin, sitting in front of her.

"My father told me you were dead," Nasrin said. "That you were buried in Zahra Cemetery but your grave was eroded or lost among all the new ones."

"How strange, cruel."

"I know he must have been cruel to you . . . but he has been kind enough to me. I live here now with my husband and children, two girls. My husband barely makes a living. My father stayed on in Kashan, where we lived all these years."

"How old are your children, where are they?"

"Heide is two and Fereshdeh is four. They're with my husband's sister today."

"You have to come over to my house soon and see your brother. Bring your children and husband," Fatemeh said. "I can't wait to see them." She could not take her eyes off her daughter. How pretty and kind she was, with her fine features, the wavy black hair, and no trace of bitterness. A nice human being. Just seeing her made her less angry at Bahram.

It was getting to be near dusk. "I should go back," Fatemeh said. The two of them got up and went to the door. They embraced once again before Fatemeh left.

Fatemeh sat with Nasrin and Ali on the rug she had spread by the pool, talking — easy conversation about this and that. Nothing serious or cumbersome. Nasrin was optimistic that her husband's lamp shop would begin to do better, was happy that Heide's smallpox had been cured without leaving marks. Ali mentioned the newspaper he was working for. It was so nice that there was this quick friendship between the two of them, Fatemeh thought. There was a definite resemblance in their looks and personalities too, though Ali had been on edge lately, naturally.

One of the women, living in the row of rooms opposite the ones she and Ali lived in, had watered the plants and splashed water on the brick ground to cool it off and the air was fresh and fragrant. Nasrin's two children, both lovely, with curly hair and plump cheeks were sitting by flowerbeds playing with marbles. Then they went inside, running around the two rooms, chasing each other. They paused to take a candy from a bowl or dress a doll with tiny clothes Fatemeh had sewn for them herself.

Then Ali said, suddenly somber, "What does it all mean? One day and then another passing?"

"Isn't it good enough for the three of us to be sitting together like this?" Nasrin said.

He whispered something strange, "Free your body, free your soul, die and be born again."

Fatemeh picked up her glass of *sharbat* and took a few gulps of it, her mind drifting to her main concern, that the letter about Ali's exemption had not arrived yet. Maybe it's better not to know, she thought.

Other tenants in the rooms around the courtyard were peeking out of the doorways of their rooms.

"Only beggars are benefitting from this war," one of the women said, addressing Fatemeh, Nasrin and Ali. "They go from one wake to another and fill up their stomachs."

"It has given me a job," Hamideh said ruefully. She came out and sat on the porch and began to sew buttons on army jackets, a job she had taken on to supplement her income.

An *aghound*'s voice, amplified through a loudspeaker, flowed in from the mosque at the end of the street. "Gather your courage and fight on, we're near victory."

"I'm cowardly," Ali said.

"Please . . . " Fatemeh said.

"We are near victory, we are about to defeat the infidel enemy," the *aghound* said.

There was a knock on the door. Ali got up and went to get it. He came back with a letter in his hand. He gave it to Fatemeh. "It's to you, from the War-Related-Matters office."

Her hand was shaking as she opened it. She could feel Ali's and Nasrin's heavy gazes on her, could hear her own heart beat. Among all the words on it she could only see, "Not exempted." She felt a painful stirring inside her she had never experienced before. Was God really a just God? Did he exist at all or was he an invention? Or else why would he take away my son, just as I was happy finding my lost daughter? It was like she was falling into a dark, bottomless ravine.

Then she looked at the letter again and among all the words on it she saw only, "Exempted." She had the feeling she was in a dream, drifting through a maze of rooms she had once occupied, coming upon a familiar turn or looking out from behind a lacy curtain at a view, at events whose meaning was not quite clear to her. Then all she could see was a dazzling light, like looking into the full moon, with the face of God reflected in it.

THE SON

Parvin watched Bahman as he went to the outside door, leaving the house. Her sister, Zahra, sitting next to her in the courtyard finishing her breakfast tea, said, "God preserve him for you."

"Anything could happen in Teheran these days," Parvin said.

"He's a sensible boy. He'll stay away from trouble," Zahra said.

They got up and took the dishes to the pool in the center of the courtyard. Parvin put soap in a pail and added water to it from the pool. She washed the dishes and Zahra rinsed them under the faucet but her mind was on Bahman. There was so much turmoil in the city. Young men were taken away from their schools and put into jail and were never heard from again. And Bahman, though sensible, was quick-tempered, a little brash. He could say the wrong thing. It had been years since there was any peace and quiet in Iran.

After doing the dishes, Parvin and Zahra watered the trees and flowers, which stood in clumps, startlingly bright, in the two flowerbeds, and then they swept the dust which came in waves from the roof during the night. When finished with all that, Parvin went inside to tidy up the rooms she and Bahman occupied on one side of the courtyard. Zahra, her husband, and their two daughters had the row on the other side. Parvin had moved in with her sister when she was widowed three years ago. Her husband had left enough money for her and Bahman to live on but she wanted to be with her sister. Bahman and his cousins spent a lot of time together and that was a good thing too, it was as if Bahman had acquired two sisters. They did their school work together, and Bahman helped them out when they had difficulties with a subject. When they were finished with their school work, Maryam and Shirin did embroidery or knitting (Shirin, the older of the two sisters, had made a few sweaters for Bahman, which he always wore when it was cool), and Bahman sat with them, telling them the events of his day or reading poems to them. Bahman was as serious in manner, Parvin thought, as his cousins were carefree. Once, a poem Bahman read to them about a stray cat cruelly killed by a gang of boys had upset Shirin. "Why should we listen to something so sad?" she asked him.

"You ought to know about sadness, it's a part of life," he said.

Parvin interceded. "But why dwell on it. There are other, happier things to think about."

Bahman just shook his head.

She wiped the dust from the pretty friezes of lion heads and fruit above the fireplace in the livingroom, which stood between Bahman's and her own room, rearranged the vases on the mantle. Then she pulled the rose-colored curtains over the door and the single window, which gave the room a pink glow. Then she sat down on the rug with its busy pink and maroon floral designs and combed her long, wavy hair which was still full and free from gray. When she and Zahra were small girls people always said, "Parvin is the prettier of the two with that hair and those large eyes," then added quickly, "but Zahra has magnetism." She began to braid her hair. This is how Jalal liked it, she thought wistfully. He used to say, "It makes you look like a teenager." What an odd thing for a quiet, sullen man like him to say! In some ways Bahman had taken after his father, coming out with strange, unexpected remarks like that. He looked more like his father too, thin and tall, with his slightly hooked nose, curly brown hair. In a year he would be finished with high school and she and her sister would have to look for a wife for him. She, and Zahra too, she knew, would have liked him to have married Shirin or Maryam but they were both already promised to men on their father's side.

That day Bahman did not return at the usual time after school. In the evening, when Hassan, Zahra's husband, came home Parvin asked him, "Did you see Bahman?" Bahman sometimes went over to his gift shop and the two of them came home together.

Hassan shook his head.

The dinner was ready but Bahman still had not returned. At nine-thirty they gave up and began to eat without him.

They sat around a large pewter tray on a rug spread in the courtyard and ate kebab, rice, salad and *doogh*. Beetles darted around the flower beds, cicadas were screaming in the tree branches. The air had a sallow color from the light of a naked bulb hanging on the wall. The familiar sight was a little depressing to Parvin, with Bahman missing.

"It isn't like him not to let me know he's going to be late," she said.

"He probably got stuck somewhere, doing some errand," Zahra said.

"He could be with friends," Hassan remarked, but there was a note of doubt in his tone. He was a fat, short man, rather shy, and the slightest change in his manner stood out.

"He likes to go to poetry readings," Maryam said.

"But he said he was going to help me with my composition tonight," Shirin said, looking dismayed.

"Did you notice anything different about him this morning?" Parvin asked her sister.

"No."

Parvin thought perhaps she had been aware of something — it was as if she had seen the shadow of trouble from the corner of her eye, like looking at the reflection of a fly buzzing somewhere.

Hassan got up. "I'm going to the tea house."

"If you see Bahman ask him to come home."

He nodded and left.

A little later Zahra and her two daughters went to bed. Parvin went outside and waited for Bahman. She sat by the door with her *chador* wrapped around her and kept looking down the alley. Except for the murmur of voices from the tea house and the water running in the gutter it was quiet. The bazaar running perpendicular to the alley was closed; children were all inside; the traffic on Ghanat Abad had slowed down.

She saw a figure approaching. She got up to see who it was. Then she recognized Bahman's footsteps.

"Is that you?" she asked.

"Yes. What are you doing here?"

"You're late. I was afraid."

"You worry about me too much. I'm not a child any longer."

"It's past midnight."

He did not reply. They went inside and he went to his room.

With Bahman safely in the house Parvin calmed down somewhat. I am probably over-protective, she thought, he being an only child and fatherless. And Jalal's sudden death, when his fruit truck had turned over, had left a deep mark that affected her outlook on everything. Bahman was fourteen years old then. For a long time after his father's death Bahman was lost, he felt ashamed among his friends, as if he were somehow at fault. Hassan had tried to be a father to him but a real closeness was lacking. I have to accept that Bahman is no child. His room is filled with books. Surely he is wise enough to take care of himself.

During the next few weeks Bahman seemed more and more restless. He had a distracted look, and his voice was high-pitched and nervous. He would hurry into the courtyard from his room as if about to do something and then turn around and go back in. He climbed the stone stairway to the roof and came back down again. He often came home late. It was like something was straining to open up in him, give him wings.

Once at supper time, when Bahman was absent, Hassan said, "I heard at the tea house that Bahman has been with bad company."

"Who?" Parvin heard her heart thumping in her chest.

"Wrong kind of boys, troublemakers."

"It might do him good if you spoke with him."

"That will embarrass him. He's seventeen years old and proud."

He was right. That would hurt Bahman's pride even more than a real father's reprimand.

"All young men go through a period of rebellion," he consoled.

Still Parvin watched Bahman's movements, every expression on his face. She wondered if the experience of the loss of his father was somehow manifesting itself in this new restlessness. If he was even slightly late after school she was worried. She leaned out of a window or went into the alley and waited for him. Then she would see him coming on his bicycle, his books in a basket, his shirt blown out in the wind.

"Bahman, is something bothering you?" she asked him once.

"No, why?"

"You aren't yourself."

"You're too focused on me."

Still the real significance of his erratic behavior did not hit her, not until later. Then she went back to it again and again, wondering what she should have, or could have, done about it.

They were having the monthly prayer session. She and Zahra spent two days preparing for it. They covered one wall in the living room with black cloth, put the throne there for the *aghounds* to sit on, set up the immense samovar and dozens of cups and saucers. They hung, above the outside door, the black flag with "Allah" hand-blocked on it in white calligraphy.

At one o'clock on Friday the women from the neighborhood began to come in, wearing their black *chadors*. They sat cross-legged against the wall and talked while waiting for the first *aghound*. They all knew one another and had a lot to talk about: whose child had gotten married, who had had a baby, whose old aunt had died.

Then an *aghound* came and sat on the throne, his long robe hanging down around him. He began his sermon, mostly about the suffering of the *imams*. The women cried, some beat their chests. When he finished the sermon Zahra served him tea, putting his payment on the saucer. He left and the next *aghound* came in.

When the last *aghound* left, the women drank tea and talked again.

Bahman came out of his room and began to pace the courtyard. He stopped near the oval door of the living room, making the women jump for their *chadors* which they had let slip down, and said, "Do you think that *imams* hear you crying for them or that God is listening to you? There are other, more important things you could be doing." He spoke rapidly but in a sharp, clear tone. His eyes, though intense, had a dimness as if light was about to be extinguished in them. His hair was wild and matted down at his temples.

"Bahman, Bahman," Parvin said finally, coming out of her shock. "What are you talking about?" She got up and went to the doorway.

He went on, "What's the point of religion if it doesn't help the miserable on this earth? Those *aghounds* go on and on and tell you about the suffering of people living centuries ago. Why don't they talk to you about the misery going on right now? One day you're going to understand what I'm telling you, yes, one day soon." His tone now was prophetic, oddly similar to the way the *aghounds* spoke at the height of their passion when giving sermons.

Everyone was hushed, listening, a little uneasy.

"Soon something is going to happen . . . "

"Have you lost your senses?" Parvin said. Her word came out so quietly that she was not sure if he heard. She was aware of an aching distance between him and herself at that moment. At the same time she wished she could protect him. "You're just tired. You stayed up so late last night."

But he went on, "Look at the conditions we all live in. Next time you're outside see how dirty the water flowing in the gutters is, how filthy the walls, look at all the beggars crawling around the mosques. You're so used to them that you don't even notice."

Then, abruptly, he turned around and went toward the outside door. Parvin heard it bang shut and felt as if it were slammed in her face. She sat down again. "Someone has been putting wrong ideas into his head," she said.

"He reads all those books," Zahra said. "He thinks too much about things."

"No telling what young people are thinking these days," one of the guests said.

"How can we possibly have any peace on this earth without religion," another woman said.

After awhile the guests left. Parvin and Zahra began to clean up in silence. Then Zahra sighed and said, "Don't take it too hard, sister. He's young and has a lot of things churning inside him. But he'll grow out of it."

"I hope you're right."

Bahman came home early that night, holding a pretty box with a ribbon around it. He gave it to his mother. "I'm sorry I disturbed your meeting this afternoon."

She opened the box. She found a green silk scarf with designs of maple leaves printed on it. It was exquisite. She pulled him to herself and kissed his forehead. Still there remained a tiny gap, a dim, formidable area between them, perplexing her. It was as though a window to his mind had opened suddenly, revealing to her a storm raging.

"Why can't you tell me what's upsetting you?"

"It's just . . . this feeling of helplessness I have that something should be done about the sad state of affairs all around us and yet there's so little I'm doing about it, any of us are doing."

"Stay away from trouble, will you, for my sake if not for your own."

He looked around the room as if to make sure they were alone. "My friends and I have been meeting and discussing different matters."

"What matters?"

"Social issues. The injustice done to people, poverty." His voice had a vibration in it, a kind of feverish excitement. "We analyze these issues and try to see if there are things we can do about them."

"What happens is in the hand of God and those in authority."

"We try to find solutions." He held her shoulders and looked into her eyes. "Wouldn't you like to see our streets free from beggars, our children not afflicted with all sorts of diseases, people, old and young, being educated?"

She could feel a menace in the air. "I'm afraid."

"There's nothing to worry about."

Bahman spent the rest of the evening with his cousins, joking and laughing with them. He put one and then the other on the back of his bicycle and rode around the courtyard. His spirits seemed lifted.

Then one afternoon he was walking in the courtyard with a book in his hand, memorizing a poem. Parvin was in the living room and Zahra in the kitchen. There was a loud knock on the outside door. Bahman stopped and listened.

"Who could that be?" Parvin asked, getting up. She was uneasy without knowing why. Why should the knocks make her anxious? Then she understood — it was the way Bahman was reacting. He was standing stiffly and had gone exceedingly pale.

The knocks persisted. There was no mistaking the urgency about them now.

Zahra came out of the kitchen. "Why isn't anyone answering the door?"

"I'll get it," Bahman said.

He went to the door. Parvin could hear him talking in low tones with some people. She and Zahra put on their *chadors* and joined them.

Two policemen were standing by the door.

Bahman turned to his mother and aunt. "I have to go with them."

"What for?" Parvin asked, her voice shaking.

"There must be a mistake," Bahman said. He looked even paler.

One of the men said, "You seem like good people. What happened to him?"

"What has he done?" Parvin asked. Her heart was thumping, sinking.

"Not anything to be proud of."

"He's been participating in anti-government activities," the other man said.

"All we did was talk," Bahman said, stepping into the street.

A few people passed by, glancing at him furtively.

"About the wrong things," the policeman explained to Parvin.

Bahman started to say something but he stopped.

"Please wait until the older man of the house is in," Zahra said to the policemen.

"We must take him away right now."

"The man of the house will be back soon," Parvin said, her tone lingering between pleading and command.

Bahman and the policemen had reached the middle of the lane before Parvin recovered from her shock and began to run after them. Her sister followed.

"Don't go with them," Parvin said, catching up with Bahman and grasping his arm.

"I have to. Go back inside."

"Take me with you," she said to the policemen, a spasm of fear shaking her.

"Go inside," Bahman said again.

The sisters followed all the way to Ghanat Abad Avenue. Parvin kept saying his name, "Bahman, Bahman," as if she were chanting. But he had stopped looking at her.

When they got back inside, Parvin sobbed for so long that Zahra forced her to lie down in bed. "He'll be back soon, I'm sure," she said trying to calm her down.

Parvin could not remember the policemen's faces, only their uniforms, but she thought they must have been cold and cruel looking, making it inevitable for Bahman to yield.

She waited for his return. There was a curious slowness to time, every minute crawling into an hour. Hassan visited the local police stations and others but no one would tell him where Bahman was. He visited some of the prisons, hoping to find out about him but he was turned away.

He said to Parvin, "I told them he was just going through an adolescent state, all young men go through a rebellious period in one form or another."

"He shouldn't pay such a high price for a mere stage he's going through," Zahra said.

Maryam and Shirin had become withdrawn, all gaiety drained from them.

That month they held two prayer sessions instead of one and in each there was an extra prayer said for Bahman's return. The black flag was kept on the door all the time to express the tragedy inside.

"Maybe this is punishment from God," Parvin said to her sister. "For something I've done, a sin."

"You've always been so good."

"I wonder if there was something I could have done to stop him." She recalled her conversation with him about the meetings he attended and how vehement he was about his ideas. There had been something disquieting about it but obviously of urgent importance to him. She could not have stopped him any more than she could stop the dust that came in from the roof. Thinking of that it seemed

there was nothing she could have done. Still she wondered and blamed herself.

A vision of him in jail kept coming to her: he, sitting
with his knees clutched to his chest on a dirty cot in a
dark, bare room, but she stopped herself before worse
images could intrude themselves into her mind.

A knock on the door would make her jump. "Maybe
it's him." When the mailman came, she dashed to the door
hoping for a letter from him. She looked down the alley
and could see children and young men coming and going
but no Bahman riding his bicycle, his shirt blown out. She
kept looking every day, thinking of all the other times she
had waited for him and he had finally returned. But there
was no sign of him, not yet.

RAHBAR

I look at the article again. "An Iranian man, Rahbar Golestani, was shot to death at the border by Iraqi police as he was trying to escape Iran illegally . . . " The news is buried on the inside pages of the newspaper, *Parvaneh*, which arrives in the mail each week. How strange that I should come across his name after all these years, that he should have come to such an end. Was he still trying to escape accusations against him, does Aunt Mahin know about it, should I write and tell her what happened? The questions rush through my mind, stinging, distracting me.

I feel Rahbar's influence still, in the fact that I struggled to get myself out of that neighborhood, that country, and to come to America, where I got a good education and became a teacher.

I remember vividly the first time I met him. Arriving at my aunt's house after school, I found a man sitting with her in the living room. She was wearing her *chador* and sitting on a chair, something she rarely did, and he was sitting on another chair across from her, drinking tea.

She blushed when I came into the room. Then she introduced us. He seemed to be about my aunt's age, thirty-five or so. He was wearing a blue suit and a red bow tie. He had ruddy skin, light brown hair, neatly combed and parted, and large blue eyes, very unusual. He looked a little foreign. There was something magnetic about his face, particularly his eyes. I smiled and then went into the adjacent room.

In a few moments I heard him saying goodbye. Then my aunt came to me and said, softly, shyly, "He was sent here by a matchmaker. Why would someone like him want me?"

"You're beautiful, Aunt Mahin."

"You know how I love you as much as a real daughter. But it's lonely for me, I need a husband, children. How lucky your mother is, to be blessed with so many, and so effortlessly . . . But this maybe is the last I will see of him."

"Why?"

"Men want women half their own ages. Ahmad was more than twice my age. I cried so much, begged my mother and father not to marry me off to him but they insisted, forced me into it. Then he died and left me childless." She caressed my arm. "Your time will come one day, to get married, have children."

"I want to go to school all my life."

She laughed in an affectionate way. Then she said, as if wanting to impress me, "You know Rahbar is a schoolteacher."

The next time I went to her house she told me Rahbar wanted to marry her. She added, "Hard to believe."

Instead of her old, plain, shapeless clothes she started wearing well-fitting silk, velvet, georgette dresses with pretty floral designs. She splashed rosewater on herself. Her hips swung as she walked and her black wavy hair swayed over the fabric of her clothes. She made improvements in the house too. She restored the chipped friezes of animals and fruit on the porch columns and above the living-room fireplace, put blue tiles on the bathroom floor, replacing the old brown ones. She filled the flowerbeds around the pool with bright asters, morning glories, black-eyed susans.

Starting from a month before the wedding, every time I went to my aunt's house she and some other women were getting things ready for the occasion. They dried vegetables, crushed pods to make spices. A few chairs were placed in the rooms for those who preferred them to sitting on the rug. And a dining table was set in the living room. The day before the wedding the women started cooking stews, rice, and other food in large blackened pots on open fires. They hung lanterns in the tree branches, put a huge samovar in the living room with cups and saucers around it. Platters of fruit, nuts, *sharbat* were set on the table as well as on the *sofrehs* spread on the floors of two rooms, one for male guests and the other for female guests. Then my aunt applied henna to her hair, giving it reddish highlights, and plucked her eyebrows. My mother helped her try on her wedding dress, which she had made to order. To that last day my aunt kept doubting herself. "I'm a widowed woman and he's a handsome man, never married before." My mother said, "He's new in Teheran, he needs a home, and who can provide it better than an experienced woman?"

My sisters, brothers, cousins, and I went to the wedding in our best clothes as did the adults. There were a lot of people there, even the butcher who had provided the lamb came with his wife and children. They all talked and ate and laughed and made skeptical remarks, in whispers, at the plausibility of a marriage between the handsome stranger and a widowed woman. To me, though, they seemed a good match, my aunt with her dark wavy hair, large dark eyes, and sturdy, voluptuous figure, and he, fair-skinned with light hair and eyes.

And I didn't see any clouds between them when they started living with each other. Sometimes when I went over she and Rahbar would be sitting in a room with the doors shut, talking in low voices. I would hear their gay laughter, punctuating their conversation.

She was very attentive to him. She washed and ironed his clothes with great care, she touched the fabrics that had been against his skin with fondness as she hung them up in a closet. She got anxious as the evening approached, vacuuming the floors, making dinner in a scrupulous way, tasting it or asking me to taste it for just the right amount of spices. "These eggplants taste bland, and they aren't as fresh as I thought," she would say, or, "I wonder if something was mixed with the butter, it doesn't have much taste." She would set the table and then change her clothes. As soon as she heard his footsteps on the cobble-stones outside and the knocker, a rusty bronze iron head, banging on the door, she would jump up and go to receive him.

Once though, as she was putting his shoes in the doorway for him to step into, he said, "Mahin, stop doing so much for me. I can do this myself."

My aunt was taken aback.

"Don't lower yourself into slavery just because you're a woman," he said.

After he left, my aunt said, "I never know what he may say or want next." But the hurt astonishment left her face as she smiled. "He's a kind man."

I asked him questions about my school work.

"It's a good change to teach a girl, all my students are boys," he said. "Boys and girls are very different."

"How?"

"Boys are harder to get to know, they keep to themselves more."

"My father likes to talk to my brothers more than us sisters," I said.

"I grew up in a house full of women, with my mother and five sisters. My father died when I was your age, about ten, twelve." He looked deeply into my eyes and said in a confidential tone, "But Babolsar became very small for me. I came to Teheran hoping for more. Anyway I love being in new places, traveling. Before I became a teacher I worked at all sorts of jobs in foreign countries. I worked on a ship going back and forth to Turkey, and Saudi Arabia. I worked in an import-exporting company in Beirut one summer." He pointed to a white onyx box in which he kept his cigarettes. "I bought this in Turkey."

"I would like to travel."

"Then try to do well at school. Go abroad to a university. You'll see different things, interesting viewpoints."

My heart fluttered with excitement listening to him.

He took me to the rose garden at the edge of Teheran and another time we climbed the mountain in Shemiran together. It was a hot, dusty walk but when we got to the top we had a view of the huge expanse of the city. We stood there until stars came out one by one and lights went on in the houses below. I had a feeling with him that evening that he could see right through my thoughts as if they were transparent, an odd sensation that there were no barriers between us. He asked me to call him Rahbar rather than uncle.

He had his bad moods when he became withdrawn, looking lonely as if he were totally on his own, not fitting in with anything or anyone around him, even my aunt or myself. He mumbled when my aunt asked him questions and seemed intolerant of my presence. My aunt would say to me then, "It's time for you to go to bed now, you have school in the morning." Later she would come into my room and say in a guilty way, "I don't want to upset him . . . oh, he's so gentle." I began to think there must be aspects of him I did not understand.

Then for several nights in a row Rahbar did not come home, and had not given previous notice to my aunt. When he returned he said an old friend of his had been in a fatal car accident and he had gone to help. Then he stayed away again and when he came back he said he had been sent out of town by his school to attend a conference. Looking downward he said, "I don't know if I'm going to last at the school. They don't like my ideas." My aunt said, "Try to do what's required of you." A strange grimace hovered on his face but he did not say anything.

His bad moods took over more frequently and I was no longer at ease in his company.

I tried to stay away though it was hard for me at home with my mother always fretting about all the work she had to do, my sisters and brothers making a commotion, my little sister, Behjat, constantly pulling my books out of my hand, and my father's random bursts of anger at one person or another in the family.

But my aunt came to our house one afternoon and said, "What's wrong Soroor, why haven't you been coming over?"

"I don't know," I mumbled.

"I miss you. And you liven up my house for Rahbar too." Then looking puzzled and sad, she said, "He doesn't want a baby right now." She turned to my mother. "He isn't going to stay with me much longer, I'm sure. Oh, I'm so miserable, my mouth feels bitter." Looking heavenward, she added, "God doesn't want me to be happy."

"Don't talk like that," my mother said. "You were fine before he came. Why do we need men? Look at Jaafar, making me have one child after another, but is he ever home to take care of them? No. He runs around with his friends in the tea house, dreaming away . . . "

A few days later I heard a woman say to another as they sat in my aunt's living room while she was in the kitchen getting tea for them, "What made him come to this place and then marry a widow?"

"And who knows where he really comes from with those blue eyes and fancy clothes. He doesn't look Iranian or like a true Muslim. He doesn't go to the mosque."

I was trying to do my homework in the adjacent room but my mind was totally riveted on their conversation.

The first woman went on, in a quieter tone but loud enough for me to hear, "Akbar had seen him at . . . " I thought she said "a whorehouse."

I felt a chill on my skin.

"Sure, a man like that wouldn't be content but aren't whorehouses all cleaned up now?"

"You can't get rid of filth altogether, so quickly. The police are paid off . . . "

Once I had passed the prostitute district after I had gotten on the wrong bus. Women with heavy make-up and glittering clothes stood under lamplights, in doorways, or they hung their heads out of windows. Sleazy looking men wandered about. Cheap nightclubs with lascivious pictures on their doors were visible everywhere. Another time, walking at night on Ghanat Abad Avenue, I had seen a woman lying on the sidewalk having convulsions. She was half balding and her skin was full of blisters. "She's a prostitute, obviously has syphilis," I heard a man saying with utter disgust as I walked on.

Then one afternoon I saw Rahbar standing outside my school. "I've got the lust to travel again," he said. "I'm leaving for a while." He patted my head. "But I'll be back." There was a cheerfulness in him that struck me as artificial. "Here, I want you to have this." From a briefcase he was holding he took out the onyx box and handed it to me. "You can keep your pens and pencils in it."

I took the box without saying anything. I kept tracing the two palm trees engraved on the box with my fingers.

The summer that followed was exceptionally hot and the air was dusty-hazy, with pieces of debris swept up by the wind. Whorls of dust rose up when a car, bicycle, or horsecart went by. The sidewalks were dirty, full of abandoned melon skins and seeds, cores of apples and pears. Only around sunset did the streets begin to come alive with men and women returning from work or shopping, boys collecting in different corners and talking, children flying kites, some in the shape of lanterns and lit from the inside. The sounds of babies crying, whimpering, a couple arguing, and music being turned on somewhere, flowed out from houses. On the wider avenues drivers honked their horns continuously.

And then there was that horrible incident. In mid-August a young girl, Fereshdeh, was murdered in an alley nearby. Her face had been slashed, it was so bloody that she was hardly recognizable, according to the talk going around on the streets. The story was repeated over and over again by people standing around and talking in clusters. Her body had been covered with bruises, and one of her hands was partially torn off. She had been murdered in what must have been a fierce fight, people speculated, their faces horror-stricken. It was established that the murder had occurred around dusk after people had gone inside to have dinner. I could not believe Fereshdeh was dead. I used to see her passing on the streets, with such a haughty, sure expression on her face. She was very pretty, with vivid dark eyes, curly black hair and a tall, graceful figure. People said she couldn't be more than fourteen but she projected a maturity and self-confidence beyond her age. She had been nicknamed "The Princess," because of her good looks and superior manner.

Swiftly another rumor started — shaking me even more than the murder itself — that it was Rahbar who had done it. He had tried to get her to enter his car and she had refused and this was the outcome. Someone had reported to the police that he had seen Rahbar cruising the streets in a car and then had seen the Princess standing by the car talking to him. My first reaction was disbelief and then anger. How could that be true? Rahbar did not strike me as a criminal. With an obsessive fascination I went and looked at the spot where Fereshdeh's body had been found. On the ground lay pinkish dust, traces of the

Princess's blood perhaps. The street must have been dark when the murder occurred, I thought, because both the lamps on the sidewalks were shattered. The six houses that stood in the alley were set back by long walkways, so shouts for help would not have reached anyone easily.

I remained on the spot, though I was shivering with confused, uncontrollable emotions, and I stared at the blood stains for a long, long time, trying to picture the Princess and Rahbar in a struggle and Rahbar beating her with his fists. I almost expected that it might all reverse itself, the Princess coming out of a house and denying the rumors.

The incident was like an avalanche — for days neighborhood women kept dropping into my aunt's house to tell her the latest rumors. She and my mother listened wearily. My aunt's face was veiled, sad, my mother's lips trembled and she coughed nervously. I was full of a fear and a cloudy anger at everyone who came over with news. The clamor of their conversation echoed darkly through the house even after they had left.

Once I found my aunt sitting alone in the dim corner of a room, looking so lost in thoughts that she did not even notice me coming in. At another time I found her leaning over the deep water tank in the courtyard. Did she want to jump in? My mother told me she should never be left alone these days.

The Princess's family began to search for Rahbar. Police came over to question my aunt and mother about him. My aunt finally was forced into giving them Rahbar's relatives' address in Babolsar. I remember how vulnerable and fragile she looked speaking to the two tall, mustached policemen. She sat slouching a little, her head down, her hands kept stiffly on her lap as she answered their questions in a low voice.

But Rahbar was never found. After a few months my aunt rented her house and moved away to another neighborhood. Could Rahbar, the man who had spent all those weeks and months in my aunt's house, commit such an act, I kept wondering. I doubted it. My aunt doubted it too. She said to me, "He was too gentle." My mother was noncommittal. She said, "No one, other than Rahbar himself is going to know the truth."

In the back of my mind I still seek the truth of that murder. And now of his own futile death.

DEPARTURES

I have no choice, I have to let him go, Farogh thought, as she went about making last-minute preparations for a farewell lunch for her son. But how can I really accept his going to a war that has killed and maimed hundreds of young men? Seventeen years of attachment, of interdependency, could be severed in an instant. Teheran was not the same. On every street at least one family had lost someone to the war. War was like a wild, blood-thirsty animal, merciless in its killing. Black flags indicating mourning hung on so many of the doors of houses. A fountain of red water, to symbolize blood, stood on Martyrdom Square, a few blocks away.

She spread a cloth on the living room rug and set plates and silverware on it. Then she put several bouquets of flowers she had picked from the courtyard on different spots of the cloth. The room was spacious with a high ceiling and two long, rectangular windows overlooking the courtyard. But the room, the whole house, had an empty, forlorn feel to it already, now that Ahmad was going away and might not come back to it for weeks, if ever. I must not let my thoughts get so carried away.

She went into the adjacent room and began to change. She took her blue dress with green floral designs on it out of the trunk in the corner of the room and put it on. Then she pulled her hair back with a tortoise-shell barrette. I should go and wake up Hassan, she thought. It is almost noon, but then he came home late from the rug shop last night. Let him sleep. He is no solace to me anyway. For the first time in years she thought of her old job, working as a pharmacist's assistant, and felt a pang of sadness that she had given it up. She used to like helping out the customers or talking with the other employees, two nice men, about drugs, world affairs. But Hassan had started to complain, "The house is a mess, we never have a proper meal." And then when she became pregnant with Ahmad he insisted, "You can't go to work like that, it makes me ashamed. I'm the man . . . " Maybe I had given in to him too easily, she thought regretfully. And now at my age, it would be hard to find employment. Jobs are scarce for women anyway.

Her eyes went to Ahmad's photograph in a silver frame on the mantle. Something about his eyes caught her attention. They reminded her of someone . . . Karim. They had the same eyes, dark and dreamy. What would her life have been like if she had married Karim instead of Hassan? Over the expanse of years, she could vividly see Karim — thin, tall, sensitive looking. She remembered meeting him one summer when both of their families had rented cottages in Darband. They had begun to talk by the stream that ran in front of the cottages. Then they would meet secretly behind the hill and walk together through cherry and quince orchards, holding hands, kissing. They had continued meeting for a while when they returned to the city. They would go to an afternoon movie in a far off neighborhood or to a distant park or a restaurant where no one would recognize them. A year later he left for America to study. He wrote letters to her in code but after a while they slowed down and then she did not hear from him again. Before he left he gave her a silver bracelet with a garnet stone on it. For years she had worn the bracelet. Then the stone fell off and got lost and the silver became dented and finally broke. Now she wore a row of thin, gold bracelets that Ahmad had given to her last year for her fortieth birthday. In the photograph Ahmad was standing in a boat on a lake with a pole in his hands. Curls of hair hung over his forehead. Farogh remembered sitting with Karim in a rowboat at dusk in Darband far away from where they were staying. His face was lit with lights reflected from cottages around the lake. Karim could have been Ahmad's father just as easily as Hassan, if judged by physical appearance. Did Ahmad really look that much like Karim or was that just how she recalled it? She wished she had a photograph of Karim, wished she could catch a glimpse of his face. She was only sixteen years old when Hassan's mother and sister came over to her parents' house to request that she marry her son. She had seen Hassan around the neighborhood — a fat, indolent looking man, fifteen years older than herself. She had tried to resist, but her parents had given her little choice. It suddenly seemed that Hassan had kept her in captivity all these years.

A few relatives had come over for lunch, to say goodbye to Ahmad — Hassan's mother and sister, her own nephews, nieces and cousins. The meal she had spent days preparing was lavish and colorful. Large platters were filled with a variety of rices and stews and salads she had garnished with fresh mint and tarragon leaves. The lacy tablecloth one of her daughters had knitted herself and sent to her went well with the silver utensils with floral designs embossed on them. The air was filled with the aroma of turmeric, saffron, dried lemon, pepper. Conversation, laughter, the clatter of dishes, created a lively chorus. Everyone was wearing their good clothes. Her nieces had shiny shoes on and wore ribbons in their hair. It was as if no one were aware that the country was torn by war. An alley cat with long, yellow hair found its way into the room. It stood by the cloth and mewed for food. Farogh put some meat and sauce in a platter and placed it before the cat. A sudden breeze outside made the wind chimes hanging on a hook on the door jangle.

Hassan was talking with others in a haughty manner, interrupting them with remarks like, "Let me explain," "I know what you're trying to say." He talked about life after death as if no one had ever heard of it — finding oneself in heaven: a vast garden redolent with fruit, flowers, streams flowing everywhere, angels with pink and blue wings flying in the air ready to be of service, some of them singing beautiful songs. Ahmad was lucky to be given the chance to fight in the war, he said. If he himself were a young man he would be eager to do so. She felt her cheeks flushing with anger. Didn't he see the danger hanging over Ahmad?

They were fussing over Ahmad now. Hassan's mother added food to his plate and said, "You won't get anything this good for a long time." Hassan kept leaning over and squeezing his arm affectionately. Ahmad's cousins glanced at him with adoring eyes — particularly Soosan, a pretty, fourteen-year-old girl, who had a crush on him. And Mohsen, a year younger than he and going to the same high school, always looked up to him as if he were an older brother. Then why aren't they as deeply upset as I am? She felt really apart from everyone. Then she thought, I have never been like all the others around me.

When she and her three sisters were growing up, she was the one, and the only one among them, who said, "Mother, why can't I go to the university?"

"University? How does that help you with diapering a baby?"

"Mother, why do some people die young?"

"How do I know, am I God?"

And then she was the only one who had resisted marrying the man selected for her. She had grown to like him (she even loved him at moments) but a part of her remained unconnected to him, to the life in this alley. Ahmad was her strongest bond . . . What good would it do to start an argument — Ahmad had to go no matter what.

Ahmad seemed strangely calm after weeks of turmoil and vacillation. At first he had tried to get himself exempted by pretending he could not hear in one ear but that had not worked. They had said, "You have one good ear . . . " Finally he was reconciled to going.

Ahmad's aunt, a gaunt looking woman, said, "Farogh, don't think so much, your hair is going to fall out."

"Yes, like my sister, one day her hair fell off in patches. She was very thoughtful too," Hassan's mother said. She was not wearing her artificial teeth and her mouth was sunken. She ate and spoke with difficulty.

Farogh tried to smile but she could not stop her thoughts jumping away from the scene. Her mind went to those days of growing up, the daily changes coming on herself and her sisters, bodily changes (when one of her breasts started budding while the other lagged behind), her sister Mehri growing taller and prettier, her oldest sister Narghes getting married, her face radiant behind the gauzy veil, sequins shining in her hair and dress. Her own first awareness that looking at a boy made her feel different. Then her mind drifted to those cool, fragrant orchards, the winding, hilly roads where she and Karim had taken walks and talked — two heedless adolescents. One evening she was wearing a pale blue dress with short ruffled sleeves, which she had a tailor make for her. Her hair, wavy and black, thicker than now, hung loose over her shoulders. She had been feeling very carefree. The other person, the person I was then, was so much more real than the one I am now. Hassan's creation, she thought.

The next day Farogh watched Ahmad polish his boots and put them on. He was already wearing his army clothes. He looked determined, even proud. Was that an act? As a boy he had been timid. He would stand and watch other boys in rough play without ever participating, she remembered. He was introspective, unlike his father. She went over to him and gave him several handkerchiefs on which she had embroidered his name. He put them in his already packed suitcase.

Hassan came into the room and the three of them waited for the honking of the army truck which was supposed to pick Ahmad up. Then the honking came. Ahmad shut his suitcase and picked it up and they all went outside. By the door Ahmad kissed each of them quickly.

"Write soon, will you?" she said.

"Of course," Ahmad said. But he seemed distracted, with a faraway look about him. He walked rapidly toward the truck which had parked on the avenue running perpendicular to the small alley.

Farogh turned to Hassan and for the first time she could see his composure was broken. But then he quickly looked away from her, shutting her out. She had flashes of herself alone in the house with Hassan, the two of them eating together and then going to bed and she had a sudden, aching wish that it were Hassan rather than Ahmad who was leaving, whose life was at risk.

After Ahmad's departure, she continued to feel the pain of that other departure, when Karim had left the country, for a bigger, freer world. He had said he would come back and apply what he had learned there, but of course he had not. He had written her a few letters from America the first year he was there, then they stopped abruptly. She had an impulse to write to him, to make some connection with him. She still had his address in an old address book. He was in the same place, his mother had said to her once in passing as they met in a line buying food. His mother had added, "He got married to an American girl, a mistake." She had not elaborated but now the remark made Farogh think: maybe he too looks back at those days. She took out a sheet of paper from a stationery box and began to write a letter to him. She hesitated. I am a married woman. But then, she thought, I need someone.

" . . . It's difficult for me to write this letter, it has been so many years . . . Still, I remember all the walks we took together. I saw my son going to the army a few days ago and it was like that day I saw you leaving. You were the same age then as Ahmad is now. I hope you'll write back if you get this . . . "

After she sealed the letter she stood and studied herself in the mirror as if she had not looked at her reflection for a long time. Her face was round, her features delicate. She was on the plump side. That and the roundness of her face made her look young for her age. She was attractive in a healthy, robust way. Odd, she thought, I've been living in hell since Ahmad left. It made her feel that she was not quite connected to her body.

She went out to mail the letter. She passed the burnt-out, boarded-up tea house, the sooty, grimy facade of an old hotel, but more than anything she was keenly aware of the black flags on the doors and the sound of prayers for the dead coming out from Noori Mosque. She paused by Jaafari's house. One of their sons had been wounded in the war and flown to Teheran to be treated at a hospital. Should I go in and ask about their son, she wondered. But the door was locked and there was a silence about it that was forbidding. She walked on, passing the house where the opium addict lived with his mother.

As she dropped the letter into the post office mailbox and heard the quiet thud of its hitting the bottom, a surge of happiness came over her, thinking of the letter traveling so far away — in a truck to the airport and then on the plane and from the plane in a truck again and finally landing at the address where Karim lived. Would his face light up at seeing her name or would he just be surprised?

Three weeks later she found a letter in the hallway which the mailman must have dropped in. It was an airletter from America, she immediately noticed. She was startled by the sight. She realized she had not really expected an answer and so quickly. She opened it, her hand shaky. It was very brief, only a few lines.

" . . . I'm coming home for a five-day visit — that's all that my schedule will permit. From Sept. 1 – 5. Can you come to my mother's house and see me? . . . " It was cool, detached. "That's all my schedule will permit," he had said. He had not asked to see her privately. She put the letter in a box, and put the box at the bottom of the trunk in the basement.

But as the date he had mentioned approached, she felt an urge to drop in at his mother's house and see him. Now she was grateful that Hassan stayed at his shop so late at night and slept most of the day, making him oblivious of the changes in her mood, swinging back and forth. On September first, as soon as she woke up, she thought of Karim. This is the first day of his arrival. I should wait a day or two before going over, she thought.

On the afternoon of September third, as soon as Hassan left for work she began to get ready to go over to Zeinab's house. She wondered what she should wear. Something that would not draw attention to itself, she decided. She put on an inconspicuous brown dress and her dark blue *chador*.

She was hesitant again when she reached the house but she forced herself to knock. Zeinab opened the door to her.

"Oh, Farogh Joon, how are you, how nice to see you."

"I have a favor to ask," Farogh said, feeling nervous. "If I could borrow a coupon for sugar."

"Of course. I owe you so many coupons, I'll be happy to help you out. By the way my son is here. He comes every year at this time, stays only a few days."

"Every year . . . " she said inaudibly. How odd, all these years he has come back here to this street a few blocks from my house and I had no idea. She had a sharp sense of having been betrayed. Then she thought, that's absurd . . .

"Have you had any word from Ahmad?"

"A couple of letters."

"Who is there?" Farogh heard a male voice. It was undeniably Karim's.

"It's Farogh," Zeinab said. "We're coming in." Then she turned to her, "Come and sit down for a while, I just had the samovar set up for tea."

Farogh followed Zeinab into the courtyard. A man, Karim, was sitting there on the rug in the shade of a plum tree, glancing at a book. He rose as she and Zeinab approached. "I don't know if I would have recognized you after so many years," he said.

She could not bring herself to say anything. He was so unfamiliar. He was older of course, with patches of gray showing in his hair, and there were lines on his face, but that was not what made him different. His eyes were not so much dreamy as wary now. And there was something stiff and alien in his manner and tone.

"Sit down, I'll bring up some cups," Zeinab said.

He sat down again and Farogh sat next to him on the rug, staring awkwardly at the yellow butterflies flitting in the parched bushes by the small, algae-covered pool.

"What have you been doing with yourself?" he asked.

"What does a wife and mother do?" she said formally, catching his tone. "Do you have any children?"

"No, not yet," he said. "I've been so busy with work. I've been teaching at UCLA."

The foreign word made her even more uncomfortable. "Do you write books?"

He chuckled. "I read them more than write them."

The samovar was hissing, giving out sparks, which hung in the air for an instant and then faded. Zeinab came up the kitchen stairs, carrying a tray containing cups and sugar. She sat down and began to pour tea for everyone. They started to drink slowly, quietly for a moment.

"I wish Karim would come and live here," Zeinab said, looking at her son and then at her. "He's past the age of being drafted."

He patted his mother on the back, in a patronizing way, it seemed to Farogh. His movements were controlled as if he had practiced them and he knew precisely what effect they would have on others. So then, was it intentional that his gaze on her was at once detached and scrutinizing, reflecting a certain skepticism that made her feel diminished? Time has really played tricks, changed everything, him, myself. She looked at him, still hoping to reach the person he had been and to then see a reflection of herself, the way she was at fifteen, but none of it came. "I should be going, I have a lot of errands to do before dark."

"Here is a coupon," Zeinab said, putting a piece of paper in her hand.

Farogh put it in her purse and got up. "I hope you have a good visit," she said to Karim.

He and his mother got up also and followed her to the outside door. At the door he said to her cryptically, "We were children . . . " Then he turned around and went inside.

"Come back again soon," Zeinab said and then went inside also.

The sun was about to set as Farogh walked back. A kite had gotten caught in the branches of a tree and children had collected around it, shaking it, trying to get the kite free. She had a mental picture of Ahmad when he was a child and would go up to the roof of their house to fly his kites — he had bought one, lantern-shaped and lit from the inside, from a fancy store in another neighborhood. She thought of other stages of his growing up too, of when his voice had started to become streaky and bristles of hair to grow on his face. How is he going to have changed when he comes back, when I see him next?

She watched the busy street, taking in as much of it as she could, as if it were a mirage that might slip away from her at any moment.

THE POET'S VISIT

Mina and Simin saw each other almost every day after school even though they lived on opposite sides of the city. They had been friends since elementary school and now they were in the tenth grade. They remained close friends in spite of the difference in their temperaments. Simin was quiet and poetic, Mina outspoken. Although Simin was less intense than Mina in expressing her dissatisfaction with their lives, their larger view of things coincided. They agreed they would have to fight hard not to become typical wives and mothers, not to marry men selected for them by their families. One way to avoid this was to refuse to marry at all or, better, to convince their parents to send them out of the country to study.

"I want so much to go away," Mina told Simin over and over like a chant.

"Yes, somewhere far away," Simin said.

"Everything is so gray here, even the uniforms we have to wear to school," Mina said, keenly aware of how dusty the streets were, how withered the trees, of idle men sitting in doorways, of the many women wrapped in dark *chadors*.

They went to foreign movies, read novels, escaping into the worlds created by them.

Their families were very different from each other. Simin's father was a colonel, a rather reclusive man. She had one brother who was quiet and studious. Her mother was a lively woman who hummed to herself when not talking. Her parents, as well as her grandmother and her bachelor uncle, who visited often, doted on her, paying close attention to her daily activities — how many hours of sleep she got, how much and what she ate at each meal, how much time she spent studying. Sometimes her grandmother would hunch over her on the floor and comb Simin's long hair as if she were still a child.

Mina's father was a lawyer, her mother a drained-looking woman who spent all her energy running a household of six children. Mina's sisters and brothers, some older than she, some younger, all seemed to suffer from insoluble problems. The oldest sister, for instance, a pretty, romantic girl, was in love with one of her high school teachers but about to be married off to the rich son of a merchant. She sighed a lot and hardly talked to anyone. Another one of Mina's sisters, a year younger, refused to go to school. She spent her time knitting, or was just content to follow her mother around. The two live-in servants always quarreled.

"You're lucky to be so close to your family," Mina said to Simin.

"I guess so," Simin said in her mild, affectionate way. "But you have other things. Everyone notices you. Look at the way boys stare at you on the street."

Mina had very smooth olive skin, black hair and black eyes, and a mole on her upper lip. Her figure was round and voluptuous. Simin was thin, pale, with chestnut hair and light hazel eyes.

"But I don't like any of them," Mina said.

They were temporarily diverted from their usual concerns when Mina learned that Mahmood Ardavani, a distinguished writer-poet, would be visiting Teheran on business and that her father would be advising him on legal matters. In fact Ardavani would stay at their house for one or two nights — he and Mina's father had a mutual friend from their university years.

The news totally stirred Mina and Simin. The were both avid readers of Ardavani's writing, mainly his prose, which appeared regularly in the *Teheran Monthly* and sometimes in the equally distinguished magazine, *Setareh*. He was a popular, rather slick writer. Simin and Mina liked his work mostly for its foreign settings and its subject matter — male-female relationships. Once one of his novels, serialized in *Setareh*, abruptly terminated with an editorial note: "Withdrawn by the author for personal reasons." It had been very disappointing to them to stop reading the novel as it was approaching its climax. It also had doubly aroused their curiosity about Ardavani. They wondered why he had withdrawn the story and whether it had been autobiographical. It was about an Iranian girl, studying in the United States, who fell in love with an Iranian writer visiting the campus. He ignored her for the attentions of an older American woman.

"I can't believe he's actually going to be staying at your house," Simin said.

"You'll be coming over, of course, and you'll probably see as much of him as I will."

He would be arriving in two weeks. Mina and Simin began to plan. They took out his books from the library and read them. They even had dresses made for the occasion. It was late spring and they chose printed cotton fabric, one with bright butterflies, the other with tiny squares and circles. Simin picked the one with the butterflies. The tailor promised to have them ready within a week.

The day before Mahmood Ardavani was expected they picked up their dresses from the tailor, then they went to the little garden restaurant around the corner from the tailor to have ice cream. They sat in the shade of a huge sycamore tree and each had a dish of ice cream full of hard pieces of vanilla. Several familiar figures came in — the boy who always wore a yellow shirt and a black tie and hung around outside their high school, and another boy, tall and gaunt with startling gray eyes who also frequently walked up and down in front of their school. These boys had sometimes followed them, from one winding street to another, becoming invisible at a curve but soon appearing again. Now they came and sat at tables not far from theirs and began to look at them intently.

Mina and Simin automatically turned their backs on them and began to whisper about Mahmood Ardavani.

"I don't know what I'm going to say to him," Simin said.

"I can't imagine being face to face with him. He's so handsome too." In his pictures he looked middle-aged, with penetrating black eyes, and curly brown hair growing rather wildly around his head. It made Mina think of a young man she had once furtively kissed at a wedding.

Finally they left the restaurant and each went their separate ways. At home Mina noticed that her mother was already preparing for Ardavani's arrival too, getting a room ready for him to sleep in, planning menus for breakfast and dinner. Their house was large and outlandish, located in the noisy center of Ghanat Abad Avenue. It had many rooms with doors that rattled in the wind and no longer closed completely. In the summer the cement that covered the ground around the house burned like fire and in the winter it became ice cold. Mina's mother complained about the house even more than usual now. "I have a lawyer husband, we deserve better than this." She walked around the house with one of the servants, dusting and rearranging the furniture and said grumpily, "I don't understand why we have to entertain him. He could stay in the hotel."

"It will be interesting to have him here," Mina said.

"Interesting!"

Mina's father, overhearing the conversation, said, "It's good for Mina to meet such a famous man. He'll be an inspiration to her." Usually stern, he smiled at Mina now. "You're the only daughter I have who cares about reading and learning. I want you to come in when he's here and talk to him."

On the day of his arrival, Mina and Simin walked back from school together to Mina's house, wearing their new dresses instead of the gray uniforms. Right after school they had changed. They each had bought a hard-cover copy of Ardavani's latest book for him to autograph.

"Do you think it's worth it?" Simin asked.

"What?"

"Meeting him."

"What are you talking about?"

"It's just that . . . it makes me so nervous."

The owner of the barber shop underneath Mina's house was standing on the sidewalk in front of his store. He waved at Mina and said, "I gave your father a haircut today."

Mina smiled. She and Simin went through the back door and up the stairs that led to a row of rooms. One was used as a living room, one as an office by Mina's father, and one belonged to Mina.

They crossed the veranda to Mina's room. They had not encountered anyone on the way and the ceiling fans, going in every room, muffled most sounds. They sat there on hard-backed chairs and waited. A soft knock sounded at the door and Mina's father came in. He had on the dark suit he always wore when he went to court, and a polka-dot maroon and white tie. His graying hair was neatly combed and his face looked jovial.

"Don't you two ever get tired of chattering? Yap, yap, yap — that's all you do." He laughed.

Simin smiled at him politely.

"How would you like to come and meet Mahmood Ardavani? He's waiting to meet you, the two prettiest and smartest girls in the city."

"Now?" Mina asked.

"Now." He walked away. They followed slowly, carrying the books.

Mahmood Ardavani was sitting on the green and gold silk sofa in a corner of the living room, holding a glass of *sharbat.* Mina's father sat next to him with a glass of *sharbat* also. The rose scent of the drink filled the air.

The dining room table was set, with plates and glasses upside down so they would not catch the dirt from the street.

Mahmood Ardavani put down his glass and got up as Mina and Simin entered. He was friendly and at ease and looked very much like his photographs. He wore casual clothes — a blue and white shirt and denim pants. Mina's father made the introductions.

Mina and Simin were silent. The things Mina had prepared to say, such as, "I've always admired your work," or "I'm pleased to be in the presence of such a great writer," escaped her. She glanced toward the window at the dentist who had his office above the bank across the street. The dentist was bending over, working on a man's teeth.

"I'm so happy to meet you, after having read so much of your work," she finally said to Ardavani. She detected a tremor deep inside, and felt transformed just being in his presence; the air around her had a new intensity.

"Thank you. I'm very flattered," Ardavani said, raising his hand to shake hers.

Then he turned to Simin and shook hands with her. Simin blushed. Mina noticed they held each others' hands for a moment before letting go. He stared into Simin's eyes for a long time, his gaze as penetrating as in his photographs.

"You two are classmates?" he asked.

"Yes. I've always admired your work," Simin said.

"I am so pleased to know that lovely girls like you are my readers."

Simin raised the book she was holding and said, "I brought this for you to autograph."

He smiled and nodded his head. Then suddenly, as if he had awakened from a dream, he took his eyes off her and turned to Mina.

"I see you have a copy of the same book. Shall I autograph both of them?"

Mina nodded.

He took the books and, sitting down with them, thought for a moment. "I'll improvise a poem for each of you."

"Oh, wonderful," Mina said, the words just flowing out of her.

He began to write something in one book and then the other. Then he gave the books back to them. "Do me a favor. Don't read them now. Save them for later."

Simin and Mina nodded.

"Sit down. Tell me, what other things do you read?"

The two girls sank onto the silk-covered loveseat.

"We read Hafiz and Saadi for school," Simin said. "And Mina and I read almost everything printed in the *Teheran Monthly* and *Setareh*."

"Very good. What are you two girls going to do when you graduate from high school?"

"I don't know," Simin said.

"I don't know either," Mina remarked.

"I hope to send my daughter to the university," Mina's father said.

Mina wanted to bring up the idea of being sent abroad but Ardavani's presence was inhibiting. Anyway, it did not seem to matter that much at the moment.

They talked for a few more minutes and then Mina's father said, "Mr. Ardavani and I have a lot of business that we want to discuss." He looked at the set table. "In fact I'm sorry to say he won't be able to eat with us here tonight. We'll have to meet someone else, a mutual friend."

Mina and then Simin got up and stood staring at Ardavani.

He smiled at them. "I'm happy to have had the pleasure of meeting you."

"I am too," Mina said.

"So am I," Simin said.

They turned around and left. Mina's father was laughing at something that Ardavani was saying in a low voice.

The girls began to run toward Mina's room as soon as they reached the veranda. As soon as they got into the room, they opened the books.

For Mina he had written: "One morning I woke and realized I was in love with a dark-eyed, dark-haired girl with a mole on her upper lip. Now every time I see a girl looking like that I recall that faraway love and fall in love again."

For Simin he had written: "Your ethereal beauty will always remain food for the imagination of the poet."

"He liked you better than me," Simin said.

"Yours sounds better to me, more grand."

Simin shook her head. "It's so impersonal."

"He kept his eyes on you almost the whole time."

Simin shrugged.

They hardly spoke about their impressions of him. In a few moments Simin left. Mina did not sleep well that night. She tossed and turned and got out of the bed a few times and looked outside. The night air was crisp and the sky crowded with innumerable stars. She could see that the room where Ardavani slept was lighted and she wondered if he was reading or had fallen asleep with the light on. She wished she could tiptoe over to his room and sit by his bedside and talk.

The next morning she would have to get up early and leave for school, probably before he got up.

As soon as she returned to bed she felt anxious and was restless again. It wasn't just the meeting with Ardavani that had shaken her. It was Simin's manner too. She had seemed so humorless as they compared the poems.

At school Simin seemed cool and distant. All day she kept to herself. At recess Mina saw her sitting alone on the veranda, staring into space. She went over and tried to talk to her but Simin barely looked at her. Her eyes seemed to be focused on a landscape that Mina no longer shared. After classes Mina looked for Simin, but she had left without waiting for her as she almost always did. Mina walked home despondent.

Two months later, on a holiday, Mina went to a picnic in a park outside of the city.

The park was crowded with many families, their children swinging on ropes they had tied to trees or jumping over rivulets of water. Women were cooking on portable stoves or fires they had built with sticks.

Mina walked away from her family to a quieter section, and she was startled to see Simin standing by a little stream with a fishing pole in her hand. She had rarely been alone with Simin since Ardavani's visit. Simin had persisted in keeping to herself, more or less ignoring her. It was near dusk and the air had a reddish tinge. Simin's face looked flushed and grave. She wore the dress they had had made for Mahmood Ardavani's visit. Mina walked over very quietly, and standing behind her, whispered, "Simin."

Simin turned around and looked at her dreamily for an instant. "Oh, you!" She grabbed Mina's hand instinctively and then let go.

"I'm so glad to find you here. I've been bored all day," Mina said.

"Where's your family?"

"Over there."

"Mine are on that side. That's why we didn't run into each other before." Simin raised the rod, lifting the hook from the water, and abandoned it on the ground. "I have to sit down. I'm tired."

She sat on the grassy bank of the stream and Mina sat next to her. Mosquitoes buzzed in the trees that stood sparsely around them. The air had a slightly rotting smell.

"Tell me, why have you been avoiding me?" Mina asked after a few moments of silence.

"Oh, no reason."

"Please tell me."

Simin, holding her head so that all Mina could see was her profile, said, "You must know. It was what happened that day with Ardavani, what he wrote for you coming spontaneously from him. I envied you so much for it. I just had to avoid you until the feelings passed." Her voice sounded hollow and faraway. Mina felt a chill listening to that voice which was almost unrecognizable.

"Oh, that's so silly," she managed to say.

"When we were in the room with him, I wished so much for you to be out of the room — you and your father. I wanted so badly to be alone with Ardavani," Simin went on.

Mina recalled that she had had similar thoughts when she stood in the room and felt ignored by Ardavani. But the thoughts had quickly vanished, like sparks. She lowered her head so that Simin could not see the tears that had come into her eyes.

"All that is past now," she said after a moment. She was hopeful for an instant, but the next moment she could see that the gap that had begun to open between them was only deepening. The confession had made it worse instead of better. A grayness, denser than ever before, enveloped her.

DARK GRAVITY

Samira woke to the buzzing of the alarm clock. She leaned over, turned it off, and lay back. I must get up now, she thought, I will have to see Dr. Gibbons this morning. But she kept lying there, tired; no, more, reluctant to face the day. She wondered if it all had to do with her pregnancy, that is, her suspicion of being pregnant. It was true that it had taken a lot of persistence from Steve for her to go ahead with the idea.

It was wonderful of course to have Sharon. In fact since Steve's work took him away on trips a lot, she spent much more time with Sharon than he did. So much of the meaning of her days, her daily routine, revolved around Sharon — first a small, wrinkled thing, gurgling, fretting, clutching at her plastic animals or balls, then the infant changing into child, going from soft to hard food, teething, making exploratory sounds that only resembled words and then long phrases that seemed to come from inside of a wound-up doll. On some days she would take Sharon into her own bed for a while, and hold her in her arms and tell her a story until she fell asleep and then she would put her back into her own bed. When she had work to do around the house, Sharon sat nearby with a puzzle or her doll house and played. Now, however, she was looking forward to Sharon becoming more self-sufficient so that she could go back to school and build a career for herself. Not that it was impossible with a new child. It was just harder, would postpone things. But that was not all there was to her doubts, she thought. It was this apprehension that the world the three of them had built together was somehow fragile, that a sharp enough blow would destroy it. They had reached a balance finally, it seemed to her, that rested upon years of tensions and disagreements smoothed out, problems anticipated and taken care of.

The first years of her marriage had been full of tension over such things as what kind of wedding they would have — they had ended up getting married by a justice of the peace — then what they would call the baby, an American or Iranian name. Sharon had been a compromise since an Iranian name, Shirin, was very similar to it and her side of the family would call her Shirin and his Sharon, and so that pleased both. Would she have to live through all that again with the new baby? In a way it was strange that she should care about her family's approval because for so long she had struggled to break away from them, from so much of her past.

She still had nightmares about being back in her parents' house, with its walled-in dark courtyard and windowless rooms on those gray streets off Ghanat Abad, with some of the houses and shops boarded up, some burned down. She vividly remembered a dream she'd had just before she awoke. She was walking on a street near her parents' house. A grotesque looking beggar leaped out of a doorway and held out his hand to her, asking for money. As she reached over to give him a dime, the man suddenly grabbed her hand and tried to drag her into the dark hallway of the house. She began to scream and he finally let go.

She stared at the embroidered tapestry on the wall across from the bed, sewn by her grandmother. It depicted a group of birds and flowers going around a circle. The birds seemed pulled against their will toward the center. She remembered how as a child she used to stare at that tapestry, which hung in her room then, and imagine in fear that the birds would exhaust the energy of their wings and be swallowed by some mysterious gravity. She had a similar feeling now that her happiness could at any moment be destroyed by something beyond her control.

She got out of bed, went to the bathroom and turned on the shower. She took her clothes off slowly and stepped into the bathtub. It was nice of Steve to take Sharon to nursery school, she thought, but it encourages me to stay in bed too long. From her reflection in the mirror, she could see no signs of pregnancy yet. Her skin had a healthy glow, her waist and thighs were slender. Only her breasts seemed perhaps a bit enlarged. After the shower and breakfast she got ready for the visit to Dr. Gibbons and left the house.

She drove toward Port Jefferson with the roof of her Volvo open. She still got a thrill driving her own car. When she was a teenager she had seen her first American movie in a theater in a faraway, fancy neighborhood and in it the young actress drove her convertible everywhere.

It had struck her as enormously exhilarating to do that. She passed houses with vast lawns, the fabric shop where she occasionally went to buy fabric and a pattern to sew something for Sharon, the bakery, the handicraft shop where she had bought a set of cranberry crystal glasses, which she loved. The dogwoods lining the streets were all in bloom, their white blossoms creating the impression of snow from a distance, and tulips in clumps or standing alone showed vividly on the surface of lawns. She was aware, though, of a confused, insecure feeling inside her. She thought of when she had just met Steve in North Carolina, where they had both been students at Duke University, and how being with him used to make her feel secure and precarious at once. It seemed to her he was stimulated by the intensity of her temperament — he himself was calm by nature, he even slept better than she. When they lay together in bed he fell asleep almost immediately, while she often stayed up, feeling an inner unfocused turmoil. Meeting his parents had been uncomfortable. She felt out of place in their huge, orderly house. His father talked constantly and told jokes, his mother was stiff and fretful. Their only visit to Iran had turned out badly with Steve getting sick from something he ate and spending half the time in bed. Her parents and the rest of the family had been distant, treating him as if he were an enigma — and well he was to them, from such an alien culture, with a different language, set of beliefs, religion. When they were about to get married she asked Steve, "Do you think this will work out?"

"If I can't make it with you, I can't make it with anyone."

They did not invite any members of their families to the small reception after the wedding ceremony, only friends

86

were present. She suddenly had a realization that shocked her — she had never really thought about it — Steve frightened her sometimes, by having so much power over her, in terms of her happiness, who she was, or had become.

She pulled her car into the driveway of Dr. Gibbons' office and got out. She rang the bell, her hand shaky, as if she were there to do something forbidden.

The reception room was crowded with women waiting their turns. A few of them were talking to one other about the side effects of their pregnancies — backaches, excessive sleepiness. Some looked listless, from the long wait maybe. One woman was very advanced, judging by her huge, protruding stomach, and she had put her head on the back of her chair and half closed her eyes. A thought flashed across Samira's mind: if I test positive for pregnancy I could abort it and not tell Steve about it. He rarely pays attention to the bills. But then she instantly knew she could not live with herself if she did that, keeping something like that a secret from him. It would be absurd to abort the baby anyway — it isn't as if he forced me into it, she thought. Still, she felt a chilly loneliness thinking of their different approaches, different feelings about it. The words they had exchanged struck her like pieces of glass. "Yes, no, but, what if, do you really think . . . " on and on in circles. She kept moving around in her seat. She picked up a magazine and put it down again. She had a sudden, terrible memory of a woman she had known when she was growing up, a poor woman living next to their house on Khaki Alley, whom she had overheard confessing to her mother, through tears, that she had given up her baby for adoption because she and her husband could not afford to have another child. Then she had over-heard another neighbor telling her mother that the woman had not really given the infant to anyone but had put her, wrapped in a blanket, on the doorstep of a mosque, hop-ing someone would take him. She remembered that for days and months she had been haunted by that and other stories of misery that spread in the alley. Life had been wretched for so many people, full of diseases, poverty, ignorance.

Her own parents were well enough off because her fa-ther had a reasonably successful business in the bazaar, selling cloth, but still they constantly lamented being held back by circumstances. Her mother always looked bitter, her father sullen, begrudging the world. She would spend most of her time in her room and do her school work, or read, or do anything to be away from the bitterness ema-nating from her parents and others she knew. It had been a hard battle to convince her father to let her go abroad but she had managed to do well at school and win a schol-arship to an American university. That had helped. Her father had said, "Go, go away and do something for your-self." That had been such an incredible experience, giving her the feeling that she could now will anything she want-ed for herself. But then it had been a struggle once she got here — she had had to make so many adjustments, pass over so many obstacles.

"Your turn Mrs. Dawson, will you come in . . . " the nurse, a pretty young woman with red hair, was calling to her. She got up and went inside. The nurse told her to leave a urine sample in the bathroom and then go into the examining room and put on the robe that was hanging on the hook. Samira did all that and then the nurse came in.

She weighed her on the scale, and as Samira lay on the examining table, she took her pulse, her blood pressure.

"What are your symptoms?"

"I have missed two periods . . . And nausea, tiredness, tenderness of breasts."

The nurse wrote them down on her chart.

In a moment the doctor came in and the nurse left. He looked weary, his gray eyes were bloodshot, his hair tousled; still, he exuded competence. He looked at her file and said, "You've missed two periods . . . tenderness of . . . " He sounded oddly offhand, even indifferent. She remembered that when she had just come to the United States she had had that feeling about most people, that though they were polite, they were impersonal. There was a reserve about them that made it hard to know what went on inside their minds. It took getting used to.

He leaned over and began to examine her. "Does this hurt?" His hands moved from her breasts to her stomach. "Relax."

A little later she sat on a chair across from him in his office.

"It appears you're in your third month," he said abruptly.

"My husband will be happy to hear it." The words sounded jumbled and confused, she thought.

"How about yourself, Mrs. Dawson?"

"I ought to tell him how I feel," she thought. "But what for? He wouldn't care, someone with his cold eyes."

He went on, "There's still the urine test. We'll let you know the result in a couple of days." He began to ask her questions about her diet and told her what she should eat and not eat. "I'd avoid liquor and smoking altogether," he advised. He told her to be back for another examination in one month. He said the words as if by rote.

It was twelve o'clock when she left the office, almost time to pick up Sharon from her nursery school. On the way she stopped to buy fruit and vegetables. The touch of the surface of the fruit did not bring its usual pleasure, neither did the warm sunlight brushing against her skin. She paid and started walking to her car.

"You left your bag," the man behind the shop counter called after her.

"Oh!" She went back and took her bag, which he held up to her. "Thank you."

The street in front of the red brick school building was clogged with children. She spotted Sharon on the steps engrossed in a conversation with two other girls, tapping her bag against her bare legs. It was wonderful to see her happy, mingling freely with other children. She had had some difficult periods. For one thing she did not speak at all until she was two years old. Every doctor Samira had taken her to had said things like, "That happens some-times to bilingual children. They get started slower. It comes from confusion. We have given her all the tests we can. There's no physiological basis for it. She'll talk even-tually." Then at the age of two, she had suddenly started to speak, in full sentences.

She went over and picked her up, holding her hard against her chest. "I love you so much, my little girl, my Sharon. Do you know how much I love you?"

Sharon rubbed her head against her chest and then kissed her on the cheeks a few times.

Dr. Gibbons' secretary called to tell her that the preg-nancy result was positive. Shortly after the call, Steve came home from work, looking exhausted. He plopped himself on the sofa in the living room. "I had a bad day," he said. "Dennis Cross kept complaining about the state the company is in. He wants me to do the tranquilizer formula a little differently. I told him that this is a respectable pharmaceutical laboratory, we can't take a risk messing around with the established formula. He didn't really want to hear me."

She went and sat on a soft chair across from him, curling her legs up under her, thinking, "I haven't told him the news yet." She had to force herself to say, "I'm definitely pregnant. They called me from Gibbons' office."

"How wonderful. Why didn't you call me immediately and tell me," he said, excited, leaning over and holding her hand in his.

She shrugged. "They called only an hour ago."

"Your hand is cold. You look agitated. Excited?"

"A little." She studied his face closely to see if he was holding back any anxiety of his own but it was hard to tell. His wary, blue eyes looked as though he were trying to express happiness.

Sharon came down the stairs. "Will you play a game with me?" she asked her mother.

"Not now."

"You didn't give me a kiss," Steve said.

Sharon went over and kissed her father quickly on the cheek and then ran back to her.

"Soon you're going to have a baby sister or brother," Samira said, picking her up and putting her on her lap.

"When?" Sharon asked, looking confused.

"In about six months."

"What's its name?"

"I don't know yet."

"I don't want a baby sister or brother."

"It will be nice for you. You'll play with her and help me take care of her," Samira said, thinking her voice did not reflect conviction. Her face had grown hot, her breathing shallow.

"I won't, I won't," Sharon protested.

Steve turned to Samira. "We ought to go out tonight and celebrate."

"I'm not sure if I'm in the mood." She put Sharon down and Sharon walked away and started to go up the stairs. Then Samira said in a whisper, "All the problems a new baby is going to create."

"What are you talking about? Everything will be fine."

After a moment of silence between them, she said, "We'd better decide which room to give the baby."

"I think the one next to Sharon's. It's just the right size."

"But the baby will wake Sharon at night."

"How about the one on the other side of ours."

"I think so." She sighed.

Sharon who had gone up the stairs was climbing down again, jumping noisily from one step onto another.

"Quiet, we're talking," Steve said.

Sharon ignored that and began to make additional noises with her mouth. "Boom, boom."

Samira could see anger rising in Steve.

"Hickory, dickory, dock, the mouse ran up the clock," Sharon chanted.

Steve gave her a warning look. "Stop, will you. You aren't two years old, you know."

It is so unlike him to lose his temper, Samira thought. "Why don't you go to your room and play," she said to Sharon.

But Sharon resumed running up and down the stairs, singing, "Hickory, dickory, dock . . . "

Steve jumped up and went over to her. He grabbed her flailing arms and held them down, pinning her in place for an instant before letting go. His face was flushed. "Don't you ever listen to what I tell you?"

"Leave her alone. She's upset," Samira said, almost shouting. A lonely feverish look had come into Sharon's eyes. Samira went to her and, lifting her up, held her against her chest. She felt Sharon clinging to her. She suddenly had a vivid, horrible vision — the light in the room changed into the distant, menacing one of the past; the house, the well-tended, flower-filled yard around it, vanished and was replaced by that dark house of her childhood. Then Sharon and Steve disappeared too, as if into a dream. Everything, brick by brick, crumbled.

When she came back to herself, her heart was beating violently.

She heard Steve saying ruefully, "It must be the change that makes her act like this, the new baby."

She rocked Sharon back and forth, rhythmically. Gradually the terrible feelings in herself began to pass and then looking at Steve she could see an almost childlike transparency about him, with no jagged edges, nothing forceful in his character. Of course Steve is a person, she thought, not a part of a force, as Sharon, the new baby and I each are persons, separate and united at the same time. Like pebbles in a rushing river, which is rough in spots, smooth in others, crashing at moments and then gurgling happily. Once again, deep inside her, the frightened self lay at peace.

THE CALLING

Even after a week Mohtaram could not believe that her sister, Narghes, was really with her in the living room of her house. But there she was, her polka dot *chador* wrapped around her, sitting in a patch of the sun on the living room rug to warm her legs, although it was late May and the temperature hovered around seventy.

The house, too, had marks of Narghes' presence — a cloth with paisley designs covered the kitchen table, a tapestry depicting a caravan hung on a wall, and the smell of rosewater that Narghes dabbed on her clothes permeated the air.

Before Narghes came, Mohtaram had spent days preparing for the visit — dusting every corner, washing the bedspreads, curtains, tablecloths, scrubbing pots and pans, buying a side of mutton from the young man who

slaughtered a sheep every few weeks in the Muslim fash-
ion and sold it to other Iranians in town. For years she
had been asking Narghes to come for a visit. She wrote to
her. "You will love Ohio. It is sparkling clean with no dust
to settle on things. There are many trees and lakes and
rivers . . . " Narghes had always refused, saying, "I have
my prayer sessions starting next month," or "Bahman
wants to get married and we're looking for a proper wife
for him." What had prompted her to come now, Narghes
had told her, was a dream she had. In the dream she was
searching for Mohtaram and finally found her, scratched
and bleeding, in a wide, well-lit but empty street. The
dream had so shaken her that she decided she must see
her sister immediately.

But there was a reserve in Narghes' attitude, a kept-in
dissatisfaction that made Mohtaram wonder. The first
night she had arrived, Narghes had inspected everything
in the house to make sure it adhered to the Muslim laws.
She asked Mohtaram if she had washed and rinsed the
sheets and towels herself and not mixed them with others'
wash in those huge washing machines she had heard of.
She would make Mohtaram read the ingredients in pack-
aged items — crackers, cookies, and bread — before she
would eat them. She explained to Mohtaram that a young
man in their neighborhood in Teheran had told her, "Be
careful, they use pork fat in cooking in America."

Mohtaram tried to reassure her, "Don't worry, I have
my own private washing machine. I wash everything in
that," or "I wouldn't buy anything with pork fat in it . . . "

Already in one week Mohtaram was falling into the old
interdependency with her sister. Every day they woke at
dawn, prayed, had breakfast, talked to visitors, went out

for a walk, came back and had lunch, prayed, took naps, had supper, prayed again.

The shopping center was not too far away and they could walk to it. Narghes would wear a *chador* and Mohtaram a long-sleeved dress and a scarf on her head. Although Narghes complained about her legs and walked rather slowly, she gave the impression of being the stronger of the two with sturdy arms and ample breasts. Mohtaram felt thin and frail by contrast and was aware that her fairer skin had wrinkled more. It was hard to tell, she was sure, which one of them was older, even though there was a five-year difference in age between them.

On the walks Narghes would say, "No one seems to be home, the houses are so quiet." She was outraged by the way older women carried themselves. "Look, look, all that rouge and lipstick she has on."

People occasionally turned around and looked at her in her long black *chador* and some smiled at her but just as often they acted as if they did not notice anything different.

"See, they leave you alone here," Mohtaram said. "No one interferes in your affairs."

"But it's so lonely, it's like everyone has crawled into a shell," Narghes said.

It seemed to Mohtaram that it would have been more natural to Narghes if people stared or even poked at her *chador* and asked her what it was.

One thing, though, caught Narghes' attention, something she liked, a pair of soft, flat shoes in the window of a dime store. "They look so comfortable. They'll be perfect for me," she said. "I constantly change shoes and never find any that fit."

They had gone in and she tried on the shoes. They were imported from Japan and cost only five dollars. She bought two pair. She wore one pair on the way back. She said they felt as comfortable as they looked.

In the evenings she was restless. She looked around at the house and said, "All the windows have the same shape and the rooms are all the same size." Her own house in Iran was full of variously shaped windows, some of stained glass that cast colorful light onto the rugs. And the rooms had different contours and sizes. She wrote long letters home and although she knew it would take at least three weeks for a letter to get there and back, after a few days she would begin to expect an answer. "Was there anything for me?" she asked every time Mohtaram went out to check the mail. Tired of waiting she wrote more letters. She wrote them slowly and laboriously with her lips moving, forming words. She told Mohtaram endless stories about the relatives, the brothers, nephews, nieces and aunts and uncles all living in houses near each other in a network of alleys off Ghanat Abad Avenue.

Mohtaram, though, thought that even with all the details, there was something imprecise and foggy about these accounts, like a distorted mirror of her own memory. She wished she could reconstruct everything with more clarity, she longed to be there and experience them for herself. It seemed to her now, after many years of living in Athens, that she had not really known what she was getting herself into when she had sold everything she had in Iran after her husband died, and had come to America to live near her son. For one thing, she saw Cyrus only a few moments every day when he stopped in before he went to the university to do his teaching. When his children were younger she saw them every day, but now they were at school and busy with their friends. Mildred, Cyrus' wife, had not learned Farsi and her own English was not all that good, so they could not really talk to each other. Feri, her daughter, who had come to America shortly after Cyrus did, was studying in Madison, Wisconsin and was married to an Iranian engineer, but the distance made it hard for them to get together. She had a few Iranian friends who lived in town but they were all younger than she, and had different interests . . .

She got up. "I'm going to get started, they should all be here soon," she said to Narghes. Feri and Sohrab were flying in from Madison to spend the weekend so that Feri could see her aunt, and Mohtaram had invited Cyrus and Mildred and an Iranian couple living nearby to come for lunch too.

"I'll help you," Narghes said, getting up. They went into the kitchen and began to prepare — cutting eggplants, green beans, cucumbers, soaking the rice, raisins and lentils. They used some of the spices Narghes had brought with her — turmeric, sumac, dried ground lemon, a combination of coriander, cinnamon and pepper. The air was filled with scents Mohtaram associated with home.

Cyrus arrived first. He came into the living room and said, "Mildred has a cold and couldn't come but she sent this." He held out a large platter. "Apple pie, especially for you, Aunt Narghes."

"You all have been so kind to me," Narghes said. "It makes me ashamed."

Cyrus walked into the kitchen and put the pie on the counter. He took out packs of beer from a bag he was holding and put them in the refrigerator. He was only sixteen years younger than his mother and had alert brown eyes, curly hair and muscular arms from lifting weights every day, one habit he had kept, Mohtaram noticed, from his adolescent years in Iran. He came back into the living room and sat on the semi-circular sofa.

Narghes gathered her legs under her. "I ache all the time. I'm on the way to my grave."

"Don't say such things," Cyrus said. "People here get married at your age and start a new life."

Mohtaram took the potatoes she had sliced into the kitchen to fry them, but she kept her eyes half way on Narghes and Cyrus. She wanted to make sure no misunderstanding would develop between them, like the time Narghes had told him bluntly that unless he had had a Muslim wedding ceremony his marriage to Mildred was not valid, and Cyrus had flushed and had not answered, maybe out of pride. Mohtaram had explained for him, "I made sure to marry them with the Koran myself. I said the words and they both went along with it. I converted her first into Islam and gave her the name Zobeideh."

"Tell me all about Uncle Mohammed and Uncle Ahmad," Cyrus was saying to Narghes. "I haven't had any news from them for years."

"What is there to say about them?" But she went on to talk about her brothers at length. Uncle Mohammed had retired from his job as a clerk in the City Hall and spent his days going to the mosque or on pilgrimages with his wife. Uncle Ahmad had had a gall bladder removed.

There were some noises outside the house, a car pulling in, and then footsteps.

"It must be them, Feri and Sohrab," Mohtaram said from the kitchen and went to open the outside door.

"You're right on time," she said to the two young women who were standing there holding small suitcases. "Come in, come in, nice to see you." She kissed Feri and Sohrab and they all went inside.

Feri dashed to her aunt and they embraced and kissed. Then she introduced Sohrab and Narghes to each other.

"You're as pretty as when you were a child," Narghes said to her.

"Thank you. I've been counting the days to see you. I had final exams or else I would have been here much sooner," Feri said.

Then they all sat down. In a few moments Narghes took from her purse two matching gold pendants with "Allah" inscribed on them in Arabic script and gave one to Sohrab and the other to Feri. Feri and Sohrab thanked her and put them on. Mohtaram thought the pendants looked a little strange on them with their short haircuts and blue-jeans and wild looking tee-shirts.

Sohrab engaged Cyrus in conversation while Narghes and Feri talked between themselves.

"Have you thought of children yet? You're almost thirty, time is running out for you," Narghes said to Feri.

"I've been too busy to think about it," Feri said.

"You don't want to end up childless like me."

"Yes, Aunt Narghes, tell her that," Sohrab said, turning to them.

Feri laughed and leaned against his chest. He stroked her cheek for a moment and then let go.

"Let's play some records," Cyrus said. "Persian music for the occasion. Do you mind, Aunt Narghes?"

Narghes looked into space and nodded her head ambiguously.

He searched through the small stack of records next to the phonograph and put one on. A soft, nasal female voice began to sing, "Oh, my love, you're like a wild flower on the hills, out of my reach, out of my reach." Cyrus listened, a mocking smile lingering on his face.

Mohtaram asked Feri if she would help her set out the food, then the two of them began to go back and forth into the kitchen, carrying things. They spread a cloth, with hand-blocked designs of camels and trees, on the living room floor and then they set the dishes and silverware on it.

Feri said, "This is interesting, an all-Iranian lunch."

"Let me carry some things too," Narghes said, starting to get up.

"No, don't move," Mohtaram said. "It is difficult with the *chador*. You've already worked hard enough."

Narghes sat down again.

Mohtaram thought suddenly how much closer she was to Narghes than to Feri with her pert, sharp movements.

Some footsteps sounded in the driveway again. "Here they are, Mehdi and Simin," Mohtaram said.

A moment later Mehdi and Simin came in. They glanced around the room, greeting everyone. Mehdi was holding a basket with four chickens, their legs tied with a rope. The chickens lay placidly in the basket.

"I brought these so that we can slaughter them the Muslim way for Narghes *khanoom*."

"Thank you, please put them on the porch," Mohtaram said.

"May God pay you back for all your troubles," Narghes said. "I can't thank you enough."

Mehdi went out through the screen door and laid the chickens on the porch. The chickens began to cluck frantically as if they knew they had little time left to live.

Mohtaram and Feri brought over the food and put it on the cloth — two stews, two kinds of rice, a yogurt and cucumber salad, *sharbat* to drink, halva, and the huge apple pie Cyrus had brought over for dessert.

"Let's sit down and eat," Mohtaram said.

They sat around the cloth and started to eat. Then the pie was served. Narghes refused.

Mohtaram said, "Mildred is scrupulous. She must have rinsed everything several times."

Narghes still looked hesitant.

"It's just flour, sugar and apples," Mohtaram said.

Narghes took a slice and began to eat it. "It's very good. May God give strength to your wife," she said to Cyrus.

Cyrus smiled. "I'm glad you like it."

After lunch the men sat in one corner and started to drink beer and talk while the women had tea. Narghes and Mohtaram were quiet. Mohtaram observed how aloof her children seemed in contrast to Narghes. There was something off-hand about them, though clearly they were trying to be nice. Their attitude toward the occasion, it seemed to her, was that of amusement. When children, they had been like all other Iranian children, dependent on her approval, thriving on her warmth, her cuddling and kisses, but they had changed. They were as cool and independent and egocentric as she imagined most Americans to be. Maybe I too have changed, she thought, becoming a little like them. This knowledge, which hit her for the first time, really upset her. Maybe it is Narghes who makes me feel this way. I must be seeing things through her eyes, for this is how Narghes must be viewing my Americanized children as she sits there looking on quietly.

Feri and Simin went into the kitchen to do the dishes. They were talking rapidly and intensely to each other, their voices occasionally rising above those of the men in the living room.

Cyrus, Mehdi, and Sohrab kept drinking beer and talking. Mehdi was bragging about how much he won every time he went to the horse races, one hundred dollars last time. Sohrab talked about his engineering firm, how the salesmen always went after girls when they traveled, and, he added in a whisper, some call girls were arranged for them by the customers' companies. Then Mehdi said to Cyrus, "You college teachers have all those young girls available to you. They want to be in your favor and so . . . "

"There is this student in one of my classes. She always sits in the first row, crossing her legs and . . . " Cyrus paused and then added something that Mohtaram, even though she strained, could not hear. Then all the men began to laugh about something, a private joke.

After a moment Mehdi said, "They don't think of that as being loose morally. I used to think every time a girl smiled at me she meant something by it but that isn't necessarily the case."

The other two laughed again.

"American girls think nothing of such matters," Cyrus said. "And why should they?"

Mohtaram was aware of Narghes shifting tensely.

Just then Narghes broke her silence, but with an unexpected remark. "Mohtaram, why did you do this to me, making me eat the unclean food?" Her face went white, her dark eyes rolled upward as if she were delirious.

"What's the matter? I don't understand what you're talking about," Mohtaram said.

"I heard what they were saying in the kitchen."

"What did you hear?"

"The pie Cyrus brought over had been cooked in pig's fat."

"Who said that?"

"Feri said it."

"Feri, come over here," Mohtaram called urgently.

Feri came to the doorway of the room.

"Did you say that the pie crust was cooked in pig's fat?"

"No."

"What did you say then?"

"I was talking about a pie I took to a picnic. I used bacon and ham in it. It was a quiche Lorraine, a French dish."

Simin came into the doorway also. "Yes, Narghes *khanoom*, that's what Feri was telling me."

"Apple pie in pig's fat?" Cyrus said.

"All the sinful talk in this room and the beer dripping on the rugs where we pray." Narghes looked from face to face. "It was a mistake for me to travel to here."

"We just finished the last beer so there won't be any more of it," Cyrus said.

"I'm spoiling the day for you. That's why I shouldn't have come at all. I will go home soon," Narghes said.

"If you go back so soon we all will be heart-broken," Feri said.

Narghes looked down in deep contemplation.

Everyone was quiet, enveloped in the tension hanging in the air. Then Cyrus got up and said, "I have to go home, I have a lot of work to get done. And Mildred is alone."

Cyrus said goodbye to everyone and left.

"We have to leave also," Mehdi said to Narghes. "But we'll be seeing you again."

She barely nodded.

"I'll slaughter the chickens first. They're suffering, bound like that. I brought along a good knife."

He went out through the screen door to the porch. Then he came back and put the slaughtered chickens on the counter to be plucked and cleaned later. He washed his hands, and he and Simin left.

"I want to go for a walk, will you come with me?" Feri said to her husband.

In a few moments they went out.

"The light is fading. We'd better pray," Narghes said to Mohtaram.

"Let me put away the food first," Mohtaram said, going into the kitchen.

Narghes followed.

Mohtaram covered the leftover food and put it in the refrigerator.

"See how these chickens are lying there, dead and help-less? That's how we will be one day," Narghes said, giving out a sigh. "And imagine if you get ill, who's there to take care of you? You know the dream I had that prompted me to come here. Maybe it meant something. You ought to come back with me."

Mohtaram could see clearly now how lonely and hollow her days had been before Narghes came.

Narghes went on, "Put up the house for sale. We'll re-turn together. Everyone will be happy to have you back. You could buy another house there or if you want, the two of us will live together in my house."

Mohtaram began to cry, tears trickling down her face as if a dam had broken. "My life has been empty without realizing it," she said. "If I had any sense I would go back with you."

Soon the two of them knelt together, *chadors* on their heads, facing the East, reclining and touching their heads on the *mohr* they put on the floor.

Mohtaram had a hard time concentrating on her prayers. Her mind kept wandering to her childhood — she and Narghes sitting together in the hollowed-out trunk of a sycamore tree in their courtyard, going to the bazaar that ran parallel to their street, sleeping on the flat roof of their house, talking, looking at the shapes the clouds made, the lit kites circling in the sky, the bright stars. As a child she had been the more gregarious. She recalled Narghes withdrawing into a secluded corner of the courtyard and playing alone with her dolls, saying endearing things to them, picking them up and kissing or spanking them, but Mohtaram would intrude and insist on being included.

Narghes had been haughty, and very pretty with greenish-hazel eyes, wavy brown hair, and olive skin. Mohtaram was shorter, with smaller bones and less striking features. When the time came, Narghes married a jeweler and made the best of her marriage. She herself married a distant cousin, an accountant she had always had a crush on, and they were happy together. He was hard working and intelligent, the only educated person in a family of merchants. He was so healthy and energetic that it was hard to believe he would die young, from a stroke. Mohtaram still could recall vividly that morning waking up and finding him beside her, his unmoving eyes staring into space. She touched him and he was ice cold and rubbery. She screamed and ran out to Narghes' house, a few doors down on the same alley. Narghes had kept her there for days, trying to comfort her . . .

That night Mohtaram lay in bed awake for a long time. Memories hit her again, more strongly and vividly in the dark. She saw Narghes and herself in their house, in the hollow of that tree. Now she recalled how the two of them used to sing together, a rhyme they had made up. "I belong to this tree, to this house, to this street, and will never leave them as long as it is in my power to stay."

She wished she could break out of the prison of this new self, and be reborn again into the old one. She fell into a restless sleep, and each time she woke she had the same thought: "Narghes is going to leave soon and the house will become impersonal, barren without her, one of the many houses on the street and yet quite isolated from them."

Near dawn, when she woke, she thought very clearly, I must return with her. This is my chance . . .

FORCES OF
ATTRACTION

Jill studied herself in the mirror. I could lose a pound or two and maybe the haircut I got is a little too short. Stop being so uptight, such a perfectionist, she admonished herself. She was not sure if she really was up to going out on a blind date, particularly with someone as exotic sounding as Hamid, a doctor from Iran. Anyway the word Iran had long conjured images of "hostages" before her eyes, helpless Americans in captivity, and this was something that she had to push aside. She went over the facts her friend Francine had told her about him: "He's thirty, just finished his residency, specializing in internal medicine, attractive, a bit short, but masculine looking. Fred has known him since they were in medical school together." How many times had Francine fixed her up since she and Frank had broken up? It had never worked out. One man had bragged about how much money he made and then kept correcting her grammar, though she had majored in English in college and had done well. Another one, half-way through the evening, had suddenly reached to his head and removed his hairpiece and said, "You may as well know right away what I really look like." Then he had laughed and laughed as if at the funniest joke. Hamid, though, seemed to fit the profile of what she thought she liked in a man. He was five years older, more mature than some of the men she had gone out with; he had a profession of his own and she hoped he would understand her drive to do well; and according to Francine he was good-looking. Anyway, she had to try to become involved with someone or else how was she going to get over Frank?

The buzzer sounded. Right on time. Exactly seven o'clock. He had offered to come to her side of the city to pick her up. A good start. She went to the door entry button and pushed it. Then, while waiting for him to come up, she brushed her hair once again, applied a bit more pink lipstick, which matched her pink button-down cotton sweater. The doorbell rang and she opened the door. Before her stood a man of stocky build, with dark eyes and dark hair, and a nose with a slight hook.

"Hello Jill," he said. "I'm Hamid."

"Nice to meet you," she said. "Come in."

He came inside and stood in the middle of the room, looking a little lost. "This is a nice apartment."

"I could use more space, but it's rent-stabilized and near school. Do you want a glass of wine before we go?"

"I made the reservation at The Saloon for seven fifteen."

"We should go then."

They walked down the two flights of stairs; he held her arm. She could feel his eyes fixed on her profile. She liked him already, the quick way he was trying to connect to her.

Outside they walked along Columbus Avenue, which was crowded with many people, mostly young, wandering in and out of shops and restaurants, and with street vendors who had spread out their merchandise — bright costume jewelry, imitation Cartier watches, handbags, sunglasses.

"The vendors remind me of Iran!" he said.

"They say New York has become like the Third World." She noticed a visible tightening in the muscles of his face.

"That's how you see Iran, a Third World country?"

"I'm sorry, I meant . . . "

"You don't need to apologize. I'm used to it." He held her arm again and squeezed it, as if to reassure her he was not offended. "The truth is Iran has been sinking, becoming a poor and desperate country. It wasn't always like that."

"I see," Jill said, still a little embarrassed.

In a few moments they reached The Saloon. They went inside and he said to the host, "I made reservation for two by the window. Matini."

The host looked at his large notebook. "Matini. Yes, come with me."

They followed him to the table. The huge room was already practically filled. Candles flickered on each table. There was excitement in the air and Jill was aware of an inner excitement as well, being with this strange man she had just met. It was partly the way he was looking at her — his eyes lingering on her eyes, hair, skin. Her fair coloring was much the opposite of his own.

A young, pretty waitress, whom Jill assumed to be a struggling actress or a model, came to their table and put a menu in front of each of them. "Would you like to start with a drink?"

Hamid looked at Jill.

"A glass of wine, red."

"Do you want to share a carafe?"

"I shouldn't drink more than one glass. Tomorrow is a school day."

"I'll drink more than one, I need it after a hard day at work."

"You order, since you'll be drinking most of it."

He quickly glanced at the wine list. "A carafe of Cabernet Sauvignon."

The waitress nodded and then walked away.

"What hospital do you work at?" Jill asked, though Francine had already told her.

"Mount Sinai. It isn't an easy time to be a doctor. All day long I see AIDS patients."

The waitress brought over the wine, poured a little in one glass for him.

He tasted it. "Fine."

She poured some in each glass. "Are you ready to order?"

Jill studied the menu for a moment and finally ordered a salad and the Moroccan grilled chicken and spinach, and he ordered the same thing.

He smiled, "You made it easy for me."

He had a lovely smile, brightening his whole face as if a light had been turned on behind it.

"What kind of law do you plan to go into?" he asked.

"I don't know yet. I guess I should decide. This is my last year. In college I did a lot of work with Amnesty International. We got a young man out of a Turkish jail — we made so many phone calls, wrote so many letters."

He looked impressed. "That must have felt good."

"How long have you been here from Iran?"

"Eight years now. It doesn't seem like that long though."

After they finished eating and the waitress brought over the check, she reached into her wallet to offer to pay her share. But he quickly picked up the check.

"Thanks," she said, trying to overcome the inevitable awkwardness that came over her. It was so hard to know what was the right thing to do, let the man pay or insist on paying half. Sometimes if she insisted, it seemed to indicate to her date that she was not romantically interested, sometimes it seemed she wanted to have as much control over things as he did, or sometimes that she was too aggressive. But he was from another country; maybe the same rules did not apply to him. In a way she was relieved thinking that.

In a few moments they left. Outside he held her hand in his without self-consciousness and walked her to her apartment building. By the door, as they paused, the awkwardness returned to her again. Should I ask him up? I hardly know him. Anyway I have to get up very early. She was already interviewing for jobs for the following year. She had one scheduled for 9:00 in the morning, way over on Wall Street.

Was he reading her hesitation when he said, "I have to be at the hospital at seven tomorrow morning." Then, abruptly, he pulled her to him and kissed her. They stood like that in an embrace, kissing for a moment. Then she disengaged herself.

"I'll call you," he said, as she turned the key in her door.

The following day she told Francine on the phone, "I like him." Francine said, "He likes you too."

As soon as she hung up the phone rang. It was Hamid. He asked her to go out on Thursday night. "I'll be on call at the hospital all weekend."

"I don't have classes on Friday morning," she said.

She found herself looking forward to the date.

They went to see a movie and then went to eat at Yellow Fingers.

"I'd like to taste Iranian food," she said.

"I know of a good Persian restaurant. I'll take you to it next time we go out."

After they left Yellow Fingers he said, "Why don't we go to my apartment, it's around the corner."

His apartment, in a highrise building, was simply and sparsely decorated but there were several photographs in rather ornate silver frames in different spots, on a desk by the window, on the table next to the sofa. Through the large picture window above the desk she could see the Empire State Building and the Chrysler Building, all lit up.

He picked up the photograph on the side table and said, "These are my parents and that one is me when I was seventeen. This is the alley our house is on."

In the photograph he was thinner than now with a dreamy expression on his face. His mother was covered by a dark cloth wrapped around her, and his father was wearing a peasant-looking felt hat. The alley was dirt-covered, narrow and curving. Very different from Forest Hills where she grew up. And his parents looked very different from hers. It was all so interesting.

"I always thought I'd get my degree and go back, but I stayed on. They need doctors there badly, and most educated people have left." He looked wistful.

He got them some drinks, sat next to her. Then he kissed her hard on her lips. In a few moments, holding her hand, he led her into his bedroom. AIDS went through her mind fleetingly and then she thought of what Francine had said, "With Hamid and Fred we don't have to worry, they're super careful, particularly since they work with AIDS patients."

They lay in bed, in the dark, kissing and talking. He helped her take off her clothes and then he took off his own. He took his time, prolonging every step. It was a refreshing change from Frank who had always been quick and impatient.

Next time they met he took her to an Iranian restaurant, Samovar, where the customers, mostly Iranian, were speaking Farsi, and Iranian music was playing. They had the specialty of the house — chicken cooked in pomegranate sauce served on a mound of saffron rice and a salad of home-made yogurt and cucumber.

"How do you say 'I like' in Farsi?" she asked after having a few bites of the food.

"Man Doost Daram."

"Very musical. I'd love to see Iran one day."

They had tea, served from a large samovar set on a counter, and glazed, cardamom-scented, yellow pastry for dessert.

"I used to buy this kind of pastry from a bakery on Ghanat Abad Avenue near our house."

She could feel him gradually becoming quiet, pulling into himself. He had a tendency to be overexcited and then withdrawn, back and forth. After dessert they went to his apartment again. This time she spent the night with him.

She woke suddenly, with a ray of sunlight shining on her eyelids. I am late to classes, was her first thought. Then she remembered it was Saturday. Hamid was not in bed. She got up and walked toward the bathroom. She noticed a sheet of paper on the coffee table and then she could see her name written on the top of it. It looked like a note to her. She picked it up. " . . . I had to go to the hospital. If you have to leave, just shut the door, it locks by itself. I'll call you here or at your apartment later. I had a great night. Already in love, Hamid."

She smiled, flung the note back on the table and went into the bathroom. She washed her face, combed her hair. She had a headache — probably from the intensity of it all. How was he going to function at work after so little sleep? She opened the medicine cabinet and looked for aspirins. The shelves were covered by jars filled with medicine. Doctors were probably prone to have a lot of drugs around. She noticed a bottle with Desipramine written on it. Desipramine — it leaped up at her. An anti-depressant drug. One of her friends who had been in deep depression had been on it while hospitalized at Payne Whitney. She picked it up and looked at the label. "Hamid Matini," and then, "Dr. Kennish." He was under psychiatric care for depression. It had to be severe enough for him to be put on Desipramine. She put back the bottle, her hand a little shaky — what would be the consequence of his depression for him, for them? She picked up the bottle of aspirin and took two. Then she continued getting ready. She was amazed how strongly drawn to Hamid she already was. He was contemplative, self-questioning, different from her stereotype image of a doctor. In fact it was surprising he had gone as far as to actually become a doctor — he was so indecisive, and after every commitment he made, however slight, she sensed a hesitancy in him. Or was her attraction to him greater because of the aura of mystery about him, making him appear somehow unattainable? Her mind went back to what Helen Brick, the therapist she had seen for a while to gain some insight into why her relationships with men never worked out, had told her, "You choose wrong, because you aren't ready to settle down. You're afraid. You go out with types who are not available, pick up subtle cues from them . . . " And to what her mother said to her every time she was going through a painful relationship, "Get out of it if it hurts you. You have to look after your own interest. That's the best anyone can do." Her mother had done that years ago herself, she had left their father. She had said to her and her sister, "I know this is going to be upsetting to you, but it's a matter of self-preservation on my part and your dad's part too." Most of her parents' friends were on second and third marriages. At parties the previous spouses were present sometimes, all mingling freely, exchanging information about their children, new jobs. Her own refuge had been hard work.

On a Saturday night Jill, Hamid, Francine and Fred shared a cab to Gestures, a new place in SoHo Francine had suggested, where you could have a light meal and dance too. This was after Jill had complained to Francine, "He's up and down all the time. Really close and attentive one day and cool and remote the next." Francine had said, "Maybe it's the usual thing, he's getting close to you too fast, so he's panicking. Let's go out together one night, I'll tell you what I think." Was the moodiness because of the depression or was it his personality? She could not bring herself to tell Francine about finding the Desipramine since she had never mentioned it to Hamid.

Gestures was already throbbing with noise and activity when they arrived, though it was only eight o'clock. The walls were covered with posters of rock stars; strobe lights trembled on the platform where many couples were dancing. The non-stop blast of music made it hard to carry on a conversation, so they spent most of their time standing around with drinks in their hands or dancing.

Hamid's beeper, which he carried with him everywhere in case there was an emergency, sounded. He went into the phone booth next to the bar counter and made a phone call. When he came back he looked preoccupied.

"Is something wrong?" Jill asked.

He shook his head. "Just the hospital — the usual things."

"Why don't we go somewhere else where we can talk better?" She could see that Francine and Fred were deeply involved in each other anyway, almost unaware of their presence in the room. They waved to them and left. They found a diner around the corner. They ordered decaffeinated coffee.

"I want to tell you something," he said in a quiet tone. "So that you know. I've been depressed, in fact I'm on medication. It all started when I heard my cousin in Iran got killed in the war . . . I was very close to him . . . It was such a shock."

"Oh, I'm sorry . . . It takes time," she said. "You never told me about him."

He stared at his coffee. "They were all fighting in that senseless war. . . . Not that it has been so easy for me here, dealing with hopeless cases at the hospital day in and day out and . . . I don't know what it is; I just don't feel I'm myself. Sometimes my whole life feels wrong." He took her hand and squeezed it. "You know, we should go away somewhere for a few days, at our first opportunity."

"Maybe during the Christmas break."

It was one o'clock when they left the diner. They took a cab to his apartment. While she was getting into her nightgown in the bathroom she heard him listening to his phone messages. She froze on the spot as she heard a male voice saying, "Hamid, are you still distraught? I've been worried about you." "Distraught." "Worried about you." The phrases went around and around in her head. At that moment she felt a strong attachment to him, a desire somehow to protect him.

She was suddenly pressured at school — many papers were due, she had to spend time on the law journal, and she was called to a few second interviews. She could not afford to focus on Hamid so much. One evening she noticed in her red date book that Hamid's birthday was in a week and she was a little surprised to realize that for ten days she had not spoken to him. She called his number at home. She thought she would set up something for the four of them on his birthday — Francine, Fred, Hamid and herself.

He did not answer his phone, though it was ten o'clock and she knew he was usually home by then. Was he caught doing some late work at the hospital? She called his beeper and waited for his call. She was writing a paper on personal bankruptcy, and in and out of her concentration the thought would come, "he hasn't called back yet." She thought of something odd that Francine had said, after that night at Gestures, "He's the champion of mixed messages."

Finally she went to bed, upset that he had not called back.

In the morning, as soon as she finished her breakfast, she called him at the hospital at his floor number to leave a message.

"Mount Sinai Hospital, third floor," a female voice said after one ring.

"May I speak to Dr. Matini?"

"Dr. Matini? He's not in today."

"When do you expect him back?"

"Oh, is this Jill? We met."

"Pat?" She recognized her voice now. She was the tall nurse she had met at a party Hamid had taken her to, given by one of the doctors. She had talked to Pat for a long time at that party. Pat had said to her, "It's hard to meet men as nice as Hamid."

Now Pat said, "Didn't you know, he's on leave?"

"On leave?" She felt dizzy.

"He left in a rush."

"But . . . where to?"

"Iran. He'll be away for a while." Pat added in a chatty way, "Frankly, the head doctor here wasn't too pleased that Hamid abandoned us like that."

After they said goodbye, Jill sat there in a daze. Is he going to come back? She thought of what her mother had said, "You have to look after your own interest. That's the best anyone can do."

She began to call Francine to find out if she knew anything. Francine was not home. She left a message on her machine.

Then she had to dash to her class in environmental law.

DREAMERS

" . . . As I look out of the window all I see is a block of grayness. I leave the room and walk down the hall. Other students move around in front of me, crossing each other's paths like fish. What I feel is like I'm a fish out of water, while they are in the water, swimming together. Life is hell . . . "

Life is hell. The chilly words went around and around in Paula's head, making her shiver. She had read the letter so many times since she had received it yesterday that she practically knew it by memory. But when she called him last night he had said, "Mom, don't worry, I'm all right." She had tried to talk him into seeing a counsellor. He had said, "That was just a mood." I must go up there and see him, she decided. She'd go on the weekend when she had no classes to teach at Hunter College. Why would he write a letter like that if he was not pleading for help?

She folded the letter and put it back in the box where she kept all her important letters — from her ex-husband, Mahmood, Abbas's father; from Eddie, before they were married; and from Abbas, last semester. The first semester had gone well enough, or at least that was how it seemed to her. She put the box back in the bureau drawer and began to get ready to go out to do the month's shopping at the Price Club, where she could buy everything at half the Washington Heights' supermarket prices. God, Stella really did a bad job this time coloring my hair, she thought, catching a glimpse of herself in the mirror. What do you expect when you go to a cheap hairdresser? But there were Abbas's bills to pay. It would be so much less expensive if Abbas lived at home, it would save on rent and tuition if he went to Hunter College. But once he was accepted by that fancy school, his first choice, it was hard to say no.

She left her apartment and got into her car, parked behind the soot-covered building. She drove jerkily toward New Jersey through the rush hour traffic on the George Washington Bridge. Some of the cars cut impatiently in front of one another, zigzagged to get ahead. She parked her car in the special parking area in front of the Price Club and got out. Inside, she took a cart and began to move through the aisles, picking up one item after another, packed in huge quantities as if they were made for giants rather than human beings — paper towels, salad dressing, potatoes, onions. She also bought a package containing six shirts in bright checkered colors for Eddie. She wished she could buy something for Abbas but he was so particular. She could never tell what he did or didn't like.

When she got home she noticed her message machine was blinking three times. She pressed the playback button. "This is the Campus Store. We have an accumulated bill of $200 for Abbas Kasheff which has not been paid. Three notices were sent to his Collegetown address but there has been no response." She felt shaky. What did this mean, where was it leading to? She listened anxiously to the other messages, but they were from two teachers who, like herself, taught remedial English. One wanted to make a lunch date with her, another called to ask if she could cover a class for her. She dialed Abbas's number. It rang and rang and no one answered. I'll just have to keep trying.

"Any sales?" she asked Eddie as they sat down to eat. Why is it so hard to talk to him about Abbas's problems? Why did I marry this man if I cannot be open with him?

"Someone bought two old army jackets. A man came in looking for a cannon to make a sculpture. I can get that for him," Eddie said in that bouncy, optimistic manner he had.

He was so different in manner and looks from Mahmood. Eddie, tall, big and blond, Mahmood, short, dark, thin. Eddie was hard-working, believed in staying with one thing and building it, whereas Mahmood drifted from one field to another. He'd been an engineering student when they met, then dropped out to become an accountant, then a chef in an Iranian restaurant, then a taxi driver, but he was always writing on the side — stories, screen plays — dreaming he would make it as a writer, with bestsellers that would be made into movies. Was Abbas simply following his father's path?

She put too much gravy on her potato and then ate an extra portion of apple pie. She was going to gain back the weight she had worked so hard to lose in the Fasting Program. She could feel Eddie's eyes gliding over her disapprovingly, but then as he was helping her clear the table he asked, "What's the matter? Is something wrong?"

She shrugged. "Just tired." After a moment she said, "It's Abbas, he's been depressed."

"Why don't you ask him to come home for a weekend?"

"He doesn't want to. And he refuses to see a counsellor. I think I'll go and see him up there, surprise him, or else he'll try to talk me out of going."

Eddie nodded. In a few moments he went into the bedroom to make a phone call to his friend Artie. She sat on the sofa and glanced through the newspaper absently. The room had a rosy color, with the late sun coming in through the lace curtains and reflecting off the red Persian rug on the floor. A relative of Mahmood's had brought them the rug from Iran years ago when she came to visit, one thing Paula had kept from that time. It was hard to explain why the marriage had not worked out. It had started out so well. They had been infatuated with each other from the moment they met at a friend's apartment in Greenwich Village. Within a year they were married. Her parents liked Mahmood's absent-minded charm. They were not as demanding of him as they would have been of an American man. When he did something that fell below their expectations they attributed it to cultural differences. Then Mahmood's mother and aunt and uncle visited from Iran — his father had died when he was a teenager. They stayed in the small apartment she and Mahmood had rented near Cooper Union where he was going to engineering school, convenient for her too, since she was working at NYU and attending night school there. His family made elaborate Persian meals for her to try. Two kinds of rice, one with saffron and the other with raisins and lentils, soup with noodles, beans and spinach, chicken with walnut and pomegranate sauce, beef and eggplant stew, yogurt and cucumber salad, an iced drink made with yogurt, mint, water, and a farina dessert. The two sisters wore veils, black cloths covering them from head to toe. People on the street asked Paula if the women were nuns. The first thing the women wanted to know when they got to the apartment was the direction to the East so that they could pray, a ritual they repeated three times a day. They washed their hands and faces, spread a cloth on the floor and put a clay tablet on it. Facing East they reclined, rested their heads on the clay, and they rose whispering prayers. They liked Paula. They thought she had the organization that Mahmood lacked. They liked her looks, soft blue eyes, curly reddish blond hair, fair skin. She and Mahmood would have beautiful children together, they were sure . . . What went wrong? Was it because of Mahmood's own shattered dreams?

It was cool but sunny as she drove to Ithaca. Once she passed the highway and entered the smaller country roads, the scenery was striking with mountains and fields stretching on both sides. She thought of the spring she had driven Abbas from college to college for interviews. He was a little shy like his father, hesitated before saying anything, but on the whole he left a good impression. He had also been a good student and did well on his SATs, so he had gotten into a lot of schools. She had never imagined he would not be happy once in a college he had so carefully selected.

She reached Ithaca at six o'clock. I should be able to catch Abbas in his apartment now because he's not on the university meal plan this semester, she thought. She parked the car across from the two-story frame house standing among many other similar buildings on Clover Road and got out. She went up the steps and then into the small hallway. A table underneath the mail boxes was covered with magazines, packages, and large envelopes. She climbed up the stairway to the second floor with a sick feeling, afraid of how she might find Abbas, and of his reaction to her unannounced arrival. A note was pasted on the door, saying, "Don't ring if you have a key." Above it was a drawing of an idiotic drooling face. She rang the bell and waited. There was no answer. She turned the knob, went into the living room and called, "Is anyone in?" No answer. She went toward Abbas's room. Pasted on the door of the room adjacent to his were several rejection letters from different law schools. "Due to the large number of applicants . . . " The door to Abbas's room was free from decoration. She knocked softly.

"Come in." It was Abbas's voice.

"It's mom," she announced before opening the door and going in. To her surprise he was not lying on his bed but was dressed and sitting at his desk with a thick book in front of him, *Introduction to Thermodynamics*, but she noticed he was wearing mismatched socks, one green and one brown, his shirt and pants were badly wrinkled.

"Mom, what are you doing here?"

"I'm sorry I came without notice," she said, going toward him. "I've been worried." She kissed him on his head.

The room with the windows shut and shades pulled down had a stale, oppressive feel to it. A threadbare rug lay on the floor. The bed was unmade. But it was more than the disorderliness. Something in the room was not right, was out of kilter. On one wall hung a poster, by Folon, of a tiny man on a street among huge buildings.

"Let's go eat, if you haven't had dinner yet."

He got up obediently. "We could go to Beat the Drum."

She went to the bathroom to wash her face and comb her hair, then they left. They got into her car and he directed her to the restaurant. The feeling of his room was clinging to her like dust.

In the restaurant they sat at a table in the back. A cool, blue light shone on everything from the ceiling lamps. A waiter took their orders and left.

"I had a call from the campus store. You haven't been paying your bills," she said.

"I will," he said, looking distracted.

The waiter brought over the food — chicken wings and Sprite for him, roast beef and wine for her — and arranged it on the table. They ate quietly.

"I have no one, mom," Abbas said after awhile.

"You have Eddie and me . . . Well, don't you?"

He shrugged.

"Maybe you need a girlfriend, someone right here. How about that girl, Laura, you mentioned to me?"

"I don't know. She has someone, I think . . . "

"You could try anyway, ask her out for coffee or a drink." She thought of her friend's son — he had met a girl in a strange way — through a dating hotline. He called the number, was put on with a girl with similar interests, and then he called her several times through the hotline number until he overcame his shyness with her. Then they exchanged their own private numbers.

After supper she and Abbas went to see a movie. When the movie was over she said, "I'll drop you off and then check into a hotel."

"You can sleep in my room if you want. I'll sleep on the living room couch. We're allowed to have guests once in a while."

When they got back to his apartment all the roommates' doors were closed, with a low drone of music coming from one of them and the sound of typewriter keys from another. Abbas took some things from his room and went to sleep on the sofa.

She opened the windows a crack and pulled up the shades to let in fresh air, put on her robe, and got into his bed. Outside, the trees looked like hazy etchings under the dim, sallow street lights. The moon was full, yellow, surrounded by dark lumpy clouds. Lying there, aware of the scent of Abbas's herbal shampoo, the indentation of his head on the pillow, she was filled with an acute sense of missing him as a child, when they had been so close. Anyway it was easy to help him then. She simply fed him when he was hungry, put him in bed when he was sleepy, bought him a new toy for diversion. He would sit at the kitchen table and do his homework while she baked bread or made supper, or he read in the living room while she knit. She did puzzles with him, helped him with his homework sometimes.

She woke at dawn. She could hear footsteps in the other rooms. She lay there for a while so that she would not be in the way of the roommates.

They had bagels and coffee around the corner and then, while he attended morning classes, she went back to his apartment and tried to clean up his room a bit. The closet first. It was a mess, filled with a jumbled mass of clothes, books, records, a broken tennis racket, old sneakers, a half-full bottle of whiskey, some empty beer cans. A musty smell from the damp clothes strewn on the closet floor reached her. She picked them up and put them in a bundle in the bathroom to be washed, then she organized the closet. After that she made the bed and vacuumed the floor.

Then Abbas came back and they went to Beat the Drum again for lunch.

"Mom, I'm flunking out," Abbas said suddenly, half way through the meal.

She looked at him, stunned.

"My finals are coming up in less than a month, I'm so far behind." He said that with frightened despair, like a mountain climber losing his footing, slipping downward.

"Oh, Abbas, how did you get yourself into this?"

"I don't know," he said.

"Maybe you're overwhelmed."

Looking out of the window, avoiding her eyes, he said, "Why did Dad leave us?"

He was finally asking. It was hard to tell from his tone if it was a kind of attack on her. She said, "He was searching for something, he didn't find it in America."

Abbas seemed to retreat into himself. After a moment he said, "One day I want to go and see him in Iran."

"That's a good idea. It will be good for both of you, I'm sure." She had a vivid picture of Abbas and his father together, years ago. Mahmood was holding Abbas on his shoulder and he was going around and around, making Abbas laugh so hard that tears came to his eyes. After a bit he put Abbas down abruptly, as if there was only a certain amount of playing with his son he could take, went into his room and shut the door. Then Abbas, as he grew older, had been the one who had turned away, avoided his father. He had said to her bluntly, "I don't like dad. He isn't like other fathers."

One day Mahmood left for Los Angeles to try to sell a screenplay he had written, and from there went to Iran. After a while it became obvious he would never come back. Worse, he had not left them any addresses. He sent postcards now and then, but that stopped too. For all she knew he was married to an Iranian woman, had other children.

After lunch, she offered to help Abbas with his homework, perhaps she could get him over the hump. He resisted at first and then gave in. She decided to check into the Motor Lodge Inn and spend the night so that they had privacy. She could leave very early in the morning and make it to her eleven o'clock class at Hunter.

At the inn, they sat on chairs across from each other next to the window overlooking a lake. She noticed how neatly he still took notes, with nothing scratched out. She could not help him with the technical material but for English, she was able to explain to him what Trollope's "The Eustace Diamonds" was all about. They worked and also talked more about his father, school, his roommates, and she managed to make him promise to see the counsellor. "They can be helpful," she said.

He said, "If it makes you feel better."

It was late at night when she dropped him off at his apartment.

As she was leaving on Monday morning, standing with Abbas in front of his apartment building, she said, "Call if you want to talk about anything."

Abbas shook his head and began to trot up the steps the way his father used to go up the steps of their apartment building. He looked a lot like his father — the same eyes, the same complexion.

All the way back to New York she was so preoccupied with her visit to Abbas that she hardly noticed how the time passed. Would Abbas keep his promise to see the counsellor? He rarely failed to keep his promises. That would be a first step. Her trip up there would have accomplished that much.

The Hunter College complex was teeming with students, a bustle of all colors and nationalities, walking around, going up and down the escalators.

She took the escalator to the second floor and then the elevator to the fifth floor. She was a little late and dashed past Heidi, the secretary at the reception desk, past Judy, the program coordinator of remedial English, saying a quick hello to each, and went into her office. She collected her notes from the desk and went out into the hall and into her classroom.

She sat behind her desk and looked at the pile of papers the students had put there. She picked up the paper on the top. "Maria, please start reading your essay," she said without introduction.

Maria began to read. "I am twenty years old. I have seven sisters and brothers in Mexico . . . "

Maria's voice was trembling with emotion. "I want to learn, to understand so many things not allowed to me in my own country." There was a feverish, excited awareness in the air that anything was possible . . .

WITHOUT MY SISTER
WOULD I HAVE BECOME A WRITER?

An Autobiographical Essay

As I sit in a room in my apartment in Manhattan, I see myself clearly coming back from high school in Ahvaz, a town in southern Iran. I am looking for my older sister, Pari, so that I can read to her a story I had written during history class, instead of listening to the lecture. My sister usually got home a little before I did. "I wrote a story today," I would say as soon as I found her in one of the many rooms in our large, outlandish house. I would sit next to her on the rug and read to her, a story expressing my anger at the rigidities at school, or some shocking scene I had encountered on the street (walking by the lettuce fields one early morning I saw a half-naked woman lying among the bushes, her blouse torn, blood flowing from her face, which was so badly beaten that it was barely recognizable, and then police arriving at the scene). I read her what I had written about our younger sister's death. A pretty vivacious child with a pile of curly brown hair and brown eyes, she was five years old when she caught malaria, gradually became sallow, lost weight; then one early morning she was dead and they carried her out of the house on a stretcher.

Pari always responded not to the story itself but to the anguish that the story expressed. She listened not so much to my story as to me. I remember the intensity of my desire to express my feelings and reactions to what went on around me and of my equal eagerness to hear her reassuring voice. I was an avid reader and searched for whatever I could find — novels and short story collections, mostly translations into Farsi of American and European writers, Hemingway, Dostoevsky, Balzac — in the single bookstore in the town. When I read passages to her, she would say, "You could do that."

She loved movies and the two of us would go to see whatever was shown in the two cinemas in town, again mostly American and European movies dubbed into Farsi. She had vague aspirations to become an actress one day. We used to stop at a shop on the main street, which carried photographs of actors and actresses and she would buy a few — of Jennifer Jones, Gregory Peck — to add to an album she kept. If I close my eyes I can still vividly see her standing on the stage of our high school's auditorium (a school for girls only — a similar high school for boys stood in another part of the town), wearing striped pajamas, a mustache, and dancing and singing along with other girls dressed similarly, doing an imitation of an American musical. I would watch her and dream about writing something myself that one day would be put on a stage, with her acting in it.

I can hear my father's voice saying to her scornfully, "Don't you have any sense? An actress is just a whore." (About my writing he would say, more respectfully, "You're just a dreamer.") In those days I wrote about my immediate experiences; now, as an adult, I find myself mostly writing obsessively about the faraway past, people, cities I knew growing up. It is as if that period of struggle has much more meaning for me than what is occurring at present. How could my stable, predictable married life (I have been married to the same man for twenty-seven years and we have one daughter who is now attending law school and has a clear vision of her own goals) compete with the turmoil of those days? Though I have been writing various versions of the same events, so many times, I still have not managed to diminish the feelings raging behind them . . .

*   *   *

When I was six months old, my grandmother took me away from my mother, who already had four children before me, to be raised by my aunt, my mother's older sister. My aunt had been unable to have children herself even though she had been trying for years. My mother had promised her, even before I was born, that the next child would go to her. This was in response to my aunt's repeatedly begging my mother to let her raise one of her children. "God has enabled you to have so many of them, so easily," she had kept saying to my mother. So one early morning my grandmother bundled me up, and carrying a bottle of my mother's milk with us, she took the ferry from Abadan (where my father was a judge) and then the antiquated sooty train to my aunt's house in Teheran. My aunt was living then with a husband more than twice her age. He died not long after I was taken to them. A few years later my aunt married a younger man, a handsome, well-dressed, well-educated man working in an import-export company. (My aunt's first husband had never finished high school and made his living as the owner of several bakeries.) I remember seeing him going into a room with young boys he claimed were cousins or nephews and not emerging until the next morning. I remember the look of preoccupation on my aunt's face, her whispering things to relatives about him that I could not always hear or comprehend. "He likes boys," was one thing I heard her say a few times. "What does he want from me?" She divorced that husband after a year or two.

* * *

One day, when I was around ten years old, I was playing with a friend in the yard of our elementary school when I saw a man standing on the steps of a hallway, looking for someone. I immediately recognized my own father, who was a thin, short man with a pockmarked face and a brush mustache, but who gave the impression somehow of being strong, powerful. My heart gave a lurch. What was he doing there? I had come to view my parents as distant relatives, whom I saw occasionally on holidays when they came to Teheran. I knew they were my real parents, but because my aunt's attention to me was so thorough, expressing her need of me so openly, I had no yearning to live with them or any sense of having been abandoned.

"Let's go home," my father said as he approached me.

I looked at him for an explanation.

He picked me up and held me against him. "I'll tell you on the way." He kissed me and then put me down.

I said goodbye to my friend and followed my father outside.

"I have already spoken to your teachers. You aren't coming back here any more."

"What?"

He held my hand in his (his treatment of me that day, so gentle and patient, was unusual; he tended to be harsh and distant) and said, "I'm taking you back to live with us. You're reaching an age when you will need a father to look after you."

I did not reply. A knot had formed in my throat. I was on the verge of crying. But it was not until I saw my aunt, her *chador* wrapped around her, her face wet with tears as she handed me a suitcase she had packed, that the reality of what was happening hit me full force. I clung to my aunt. "I don't want to go," I said.

"I don't want you to go," she whispered to me. "But what can I do if your father insists on taking you back?"

What she was telling me was true: she had no legal right to me. But I have often wondered, had she not been so afraid of men or so passive, a woman in a vulnerable position, whether she would have been able to persuade my father to let her keep me. From then on I saw my aunt several months out of the year, when she came and stayed with us in Ahvaz (where my parents had moved and where my father had established himself in private practice as a lawyer), or when I went to Teheran and spent the summer with her. After all these years I am still aware of the longing of wanting to be with her, of having been cruelly ripped apart from her.

As we sat on the airplane, my father repeated again, "You need a father to look after you." I nodded shyly, trying to fight back my tears. I was in a daze as we got off the plane, as we went through the dusty streets lined with palm trees, with the smell of oil in the air from the refineries, and then entered the arid courtyard of our house. My mother was sitting at the edge of the pool in the middle of the courtyard, talking to the old live-in servant. She was wearing a jersey dress, her hair was set in a permanent, and her lips were red with lipstick (I already missed my aunt's face, free from makeup, her long, naturally wavy hair).

"Oh, you're here," my mother said, getting up and coming over to me. She leaned over and embraced me — I was keenly aware of how tentative her touch was, compared to my aunt's firm, sturdy arms around me. My mother stepped back, and, scrutinizing me, she said, "That dress is loose on you."

I blushed. I was wearing a checkered, orange-and-yellow dress that my aunt and I had carefully picked out in a shop near her house.

Then my mother quickly went back to talking to the servant in an agitated tone, instructing him about his chores for the day — how much fish to buy, which rooms to clean, to make sure to get new mosquito repellents.

I was grateful when my sister Pari came over and, taking my hand, led me into her room. We talked incessantly on that afternoon, and it seemed we never stopped. "Mother is too absorbed in too many things to pay much attention to any one of us," she said, attempting to comfort me against my mother's cool greeting. From her intense focus on me, it seemed she had been lonely in the middle of her own family.

* * *

So I had to adjust to a new set of parents with very different values from my aunt's. My parents, having lived in Ahvaz and Abadan, cities filled with foreigners employed by the oil refineries, were in some ways Westernized, did not practice any religion, whereas my aunt was old-fashioned and staunchly religious. I had to learn to live with siblings — two older brothers, two older sisters, and one younger sister. I had to adjust to a new school in the middle of the year, try to make new friends.

Our house overlooked a busy square lined by food shops, tea houses. Horse carts were parked in one corner along with taxis. In the morning Arab women would sit on the sidewalk and sell milk, butter, and cheese which they kept in large pots set in front of them. One of the two cinemas in town was on that square. The air was always filled with a variety of sounds — Arabic and Farsi spoken by vendors advertising their merchandise, Western music from the cinema, prayers from the nearby mosques.

The house had more than a dozen rooms, set on two floors. All the children had their rooms upstairs, but there was nothing about the rooms to indicate that they belonged to children or teenagers — no toys, no posters on the walls, no color in the furniture. It was as if we were not allowed to be young, indulge in whimsical or frivolous activities or tastes. My room was next to Pari's, but we often slept together in one of our rooms, talking, confiding in bed. My two brothers, the oldest children, left a year or two after I came to live with my parents, so I barely saw them or got to know them then. When my aunt visited, sometimes along with my grandmother, who lived with her in her house then, she would sleep in my room. Again, as when I was a child, I would keep her up asking her to tell me stories. Legends, fairy tales, and the true stories of our neighbors' lives were all told to me by my aunt in the same slow, formal way, with beginnings, climaxes, and morals at the end. And all were equally riveting, equally believable.

Though we had all that space in the house to move around in, I was always aware of the air being choked somehow, with my father's dominant personality trying to impose his ideas and thoughts on us and my mother always complaining. Her complaints usually had to do with daily aggravations, how the servant spent too much time playing with pigeons instead of doing his work, the fish being too smoky tasting, but sometimes her complaints had to do with my father. I overheard her say to my aunt, on one of her visits, "He's been staying out late at that nightclub with those belly dancers." She cried when my father left on business trips. "I know what he's doing," she'd say.

My father, though not as mocking of my writing as he was of my sister's aspirations to act, was suspicious and afraid of what the written word could do. He occasionally eavesdropped as I sat at my desk writing or reading. He took away from me a novel by Maxim Gorky called *The Mother* and tore it into pieces. "Where did you get that communistic filth? I could lose my license if my daughter is caught reading a book like that." In fact, I had bought it from a bookstore which occasionally would smuggle a book in against censorship. Communism was considered the enemy of the country at the time. One female teacher I admired at my high school was arrested on the charge that she was spreading "communistic" ideas in the school, the word being a catch-all for anything even remotely progressive or liberal.

* * *

At school I made one close friend. The two of us would walk around the schoolyard, wearing our gray uniforms, fear of the teachers in our hearts (obedience, subservience, to mostly male teachers was the mode), and talk obsessively about our plans for escape from the narrow confinement of that town, the life prescribed for us: graduating from high school, marrying someone selected by our parents, having a lot of children.

"I want to become a writer," I said.

"I want to become a ballet dancer," she said.

Once a famous Iranian writer whose fiction she and I read avidly was coming to town, and I found out, to my excited amazement, that he would be visiting my father one afternoon to discuss a legal matter. My father, after looking through some of his books, promised to let me and Nazan meet him. Nazan and I started to plan for his visit. Each of us bought a new dress, each a copy of his latest novel to ask him to autograph. The novel was about a young girl at college in France, falling in love with her professor, a man much older than herself, who treats her as if she were a child, not taking her attraction to him seriously. I read the book twice, and some of the passages several times. How could he make these characters so real?

When the afternoon finally arrived, Nazan and I waited in my room for my father to call us in. As we entered the room where the writer was sitting, I felt as if I were going into a magnetic field. We sat across from him and he asked us questions about ourselves, smiling at us in a patronizing way, like the professor's attitude toward the young girl in the novel. Then we gave him the books to autograph. As soon as we left the room, Nazan and I opened the books to see what he had written for each of us. I have no memory of what he actually wrote, but recently I wove a story around it, how his two autographs, one more complimentary than the other, break up the friendship between the two girls. I called it "A Poet's Visit," and it became the first story I published in a commercial magazine.

Not long after that visit I managed to convince my parents to let me go to the United States to study. They agreed to it, I think partly because they were afraid that, with the degree of restlessness I showed, I would get myself into trouble somehow or other. It was also made easier since my brothers, in the United States themselves, managed to get me a generous scholarship that paid board and tuition, at a small southern women's college. And Nazan also did a similar thing, following her brothers to England.

The closeness Pari and I had sustained itself throughout the years I was at my parents' house — I saw her graduate from high school, get married to a wealthy man in town, have a baby, a son she had to give up when she got divorced from him. (The custody of the child automatically went to the husband even when, as in my sister's case, the grounds for divorce were his cruelty to her — he put a lit cigarette to her skin, she said.)

The closeness lasted during my early years in college in the United States. At that time she had remarried; she married this husband, she confided in me, mainly to get out of the grip of my parents who never stopped blaming her for the divorce — my father had screamed at her almost daily, "You're ruining your whole life, and bringing disgrace to your family," and my mother repeatedly scolded her for being "foolish" and "impractical" to give up all that wealth. (To get a divorce she also had to give up all claim to her husband's money.) Our closeness was ruptured by a tragedy that remains painfully in the background of my life: she began to have manic-depressive episodes, making communication with her nearly impossible at times. The illness led to a second divorce and landed her in a mental hospital in Teheran, where she will probably spend at least part of each year, maybe the rest of her life (a horrible fate for me to come to terms with). In the last conversation I had with her, long-distance from New York to Teheran, when she was in a period of relative calm and lucidity, she asked me, "Are you still writing? Will you send me the last thing you wrote?"

In college I withdrew for periods of time every day and wrote. Occasionally I would mail a piece to Pari and wait eagerly for her response. But I did not think I would make writing my profession. I was eager to be independent and refused to plunge into an occupation that entails no guarantees of publication or financial support. So I studied psychology. I met my American husband right after college (now he teaches psychology at a university). Only when home with a baby was I able to justify spending some time every day writing fiction.

I began to take writing courses. In one taught by Richard Humphreys at Columbia University's General Studies, I wrote three one-page sketches, which became my first publication in a small literary magazine. One was a story I had heard from my aunt about a woman who abandoned her blind child in the desert because she was afraid a man she had met would not marry her otherwise; another was about the live-in servant at my parents' house, an illiterate man from the villages who asked me daily to read over and over again from an adventure book he had; the third one was about an insane woman tied by her family to a porch railing in their house — I had seen her myself from the roof of my aunt's house. In a course I took with Donald Barthelme at City College I wrote about my younger sister who died, and that was another one of my early publications. My first visit home after twelve years of absence was the inspiration for my first published novel, *Foreigner*, which I wrote on a Stegner Fellowship at Stanford University. The crumbling marriage of my second sister (with whom Pari and I were not as close, partly because she was not as restless as we were), combined with my own adolescent dreams and desires to escape into a different culture, constituted the core of my second novel, *Married to a Stranger*.

* * *

There is another reason I am drawn to writing about my past: it has to do with a desire to bring into the present a reality that no longer exists. The differences between the Iranian and American cultures are so vast that in order for me to have adjusted to the American way of life I have had to suppress, without always being conscious of it, much of my own childhood and upbringing. Sometimes I wake in the middle of the night with a nightmare that my past has vanished altogether and I am floating unanchored. I get out of the bed and begin to write. Then it is all with me again. I can see Pari's face radiant, she is wearing a tight red dress, drawing the eyes of the passersby to herself, the pretty daughter of a well-known lawyer in town. And I see myself — intense, shy, wearing a white cotton dress with butterfly designs on it — holding on to her arm as we walk across the square. I can see her following a man into a room of a film studio and myself waiting for her in the reception area, see her coming out, her face all flushed, and telling me, as we get to the street, "He wanted me to take my clothes off." I am sitting with her at the edge of the pool in the middle of the courtyard of our house, frogs jumping in and out of the water, bats darting back and forth under a canopy on the other side, telling her about something that happened at school. I can see her in a wedding gown, sitting next to her dark-suited husband among the guests in the large, brightly decorated salon of our house, her face reflecting a vague dreaminess and discontent.

I am lying next to my aunt and she is telling me stories.

I keep demanding, as she is about to fall asleep, "Tell me another one."

I am coming home from school with other girls, all of us in uniforms, passing through a bazaar full of food shops, clusters of smoked fish, fresh dates, bananas hanging on the doors; through a small park filled with palm trees and a little café where we sat sometimes to have ice cream; then through narrow, cobblestoned streets, followed occasionally by boys from the other high school who would come close and furtively brush their arms against us or sneak a letter into our hands, expressing a desire to meet us secretly somewhere. Coming home and being hit by loneliness if Pari is not there. My mother, remote and agitated, going from room to room, trying to put everything in order, or sweating over her cooking in the kitchen, my father talking in mysterious tones with a client behind the shut doors of the large upstairs room he uses as his office. Standing on the balcony with Pari and talking and laughing about the boys passing by, boys whom we know by sight and have classified as, "the handsome but conceited one," "the one who's trying to imitate Alan Delon," "the one with the tiny eyes and funny-looking head." Reaching over to the tall palm tree on the street and picking golden, fresh dates and eating them. . . . All that becomes a part of me again though the scene before me is of Manhattan high-rises, some of their windows still lit at late hours of the night.

* * *

In addition to writing fiction, I also teach fiction at various universities. There is one piece of advice that I am always confident to give to the students: write about subjects that you are obsessed with or fascinated by, that matter deeply to yourself.

Will I myself ever run out of steam writing about my past? It seems to me I could write indefinitely drawing from that period — about my mother who married at the age of twelve and had ten children (three of them died), whose oldest son is only fifteen years younger than herself; about my aunt's suffering with her two husbands, her yearnings for a child in a culture where a woman's life is meaningless without children; about various aspects of my sisters' and brothers' lives; about all the young girls I grew up with, some of them becoming trapped in bad marriages arranged for them, some of them with enough determination to get away to freer worlds. Then I could go back and expand some of those early brief sketches and short stories and bring to them new perspectives I have gained through writing and living longer.

There seems to be no end to the material I can draw from. But one question is always with me, haunts me. Would I have become a writer without Pari's encouragement? The question is always followed by painful regret that I have not been able to give her anything as sustaining in return. She, like myself, was always looking for escape from the circumscribed roles set for her as a woman in a culture that discriminates against them so grossly. In what way do her flights into mental illness correspond to my flights into the fantasy world of fiction? For though I draw from experience, much of what I write still has to be imagined, fabricated, distorted. When Pari looks at her hand and says, "It's turning black from the lotion you sent to me," or when she burns any money she gets hold of, saying, "I can always make more of them," is she trying to say something else?

CITY LIGHTS PUBLICATIONS

Eberhardt, Isabelle. DEPARTURES: Selected Writings
Eberhardt, Isabelle. THE OBLIVION SEEKERS
Eidus, Janice. VITO LOVES GERALDINE
Fenollosa, Ernest. CHINESE WRITTEN CHARACTER AS A MEDIUM
    FOR POETRY
Ferlinghetti, L. ed., ENDS & BEGINNINGS (City Lights Review #6)
Ferlinghetti, Lawrence. PICTURES OF THE GONE WORLD
Ferlinghetti, Lawrence. SEVEN DAYS IN NICARAGUA LIBRE
Finley, Karen. SHOCK TREATMENT
Ford, Charles Henri. OUT OF THE LABYRINTH: Selected Poems
Franzen, Cola, transl. POEMS OF ARAB ANDALUSIA
García Lorca, Federico. BARBAROUS NIGHTS: Legends & Plays
García Lorca, Federico. ODE TO WALT WHITMAN & OTHER POEMS
García Lorca, Federico. POEM OF THE DEEP SONG
Gil de Biedma, Jaime. LONGING: SELECTED POEMS
Ginsberg, Allen. HOWL & OTHER POEMS
Ginsberg, Allen. KADDISH & OTHER POEMS
Ginsberg, Allen. REALITY SANDWICHES
Ginsberg, Allen. PLANET NEWS
Ginsberg, Allen. THE FALL OF AMERICA
Ginsberg, Allen. MIND BREATHS
Ginsberg, Allen. PLUTONIAN ODE
Goethe, J. W. von. TALES FOR TRANSFORMATION
Hayton-Keeva, Sally, ed. VALIANT WOMEN IN WAR AND EXILE
Heider, Ulrike. ANARCHISM: Left Right & Green
Herron, Don. THE DASHIELL HAMMETT TOUR: A Guidebook
Herron, Don. THE LITERARY WORLD OF SAN FRANCISCO
Higman, Perry, tr. LOVE POEMS FROM SPAIN AND SPANISH
    AMERICA
Jaffe, Harold. EROS: ANTI-EROS
Jenkins, Edith. AGAINST A FIELD SINISTER
Katzenberger, Elaine, ed. FIRST WORLD HA HA HA!
Kerouac, Jack. BOOK OF DREAMS
Kerouac, Jack. POMES ALL SIZES
Kerouac, Jack. SCATTERED POEMS
Kerouac, Jack. SCRIPTURE OF THE GOLDEN ETERNITY
Lacarrière, Jacques. THE GNOSTICS
La Duke, Betty. COMPAÑERAS
La Loca. ADVENTURES ON THE ISLE OF ADOLESCENCE
Lamantia, Philip. MEADOWLARK WEST
Laughlin, James. SELECTED POEMS: 1935-1985
Le Brun, Annie. SADE: On the Brink of the Abyss
Lowry, Malcolm. SELECTED POEMS
Mackey, Nathaniel. SCHOOL OF UDHRA
Marcelin, Philippe-Thoby. THE BEAST OF THE HAITIAN HILLS
Masereel, Frans. PASSIONATE JOURNEY
Mayakovsky, Vladimir. LISTEN! EARLY POEMS

CITY LIGHTS MAIL ORDER
Order books from our free catalog:

all books from
CITY LIGHTS PUBLISHERS
and more

write to:
CITY LIGHTS MAIL ORDER
261 COLUMBUS AVENUE
SAN FRANCISCO, CA 94133
or fax your request to
[415] 362-4921